Attack
– in the –
Rye Grass

Trailblazer Books

Also by Dave and Neta Jackson

Attack
– in the –
Rye Grass

Dave & Neta Jackson

Illustrated by Julian Jackson

BETHANY HOUSE PUBLISHERS
MINNEAPOLIS, MINNESOTA 55438

Inside illustrations by Julian Jackson
Cover design and illustration by Catherine Reishus McLaughlin

Published by Bethany House Publishers
A Ministry of Bethany Fellowship, Inc.
11300 Hampshire Avenue South
Minneapolis, Minnesota 55438

Printed in the United States of America

Library of Congress Cataloging-in-Publication Data

Jackson, Dave.
    Attack in the rye grass / Dave Jackson, Neta Jackson.
        p.   cm. — (Trailblazer books)
    Includes bibliographical references.
    Summary: In 1843, twelve-year-old Perrin joins his aunt and
uncle, well-known missionaries Dr. Marcus and Narcissa
Whitman, in the Oregon Territory where they live with the Nez
Perce and Cayuse Indians.

    1. Whitman, Marcus, 1802–1847—Juvenile fiction.
2. Whitman, Narcissa Prentiss, 1808–1847—Juvenile fiction.
[1. Whitman, Marcus, 1802–1847—Fiction. 2. Whitman,
Narcissa Prentiss, 1808–1847—Fiction. 3. Oregon—History—To
1859—Fiction. 4. Missionaries—Fiction.] I. Jackson, Neta.
II. Title. III. Series.
PZ7.J132418At   1994
[Fic]—dc20   94–7589
ISBN 1–55661–273–7   CIP
                                    AC

All the named characters and major events in this book are real. However, the time the story covers has been condensed. Perrin arrived in Waiilatpu in 1843, but the attack did not occur until 1847. Also, most of Perrin and Shikam's personal involvement in the events of the story are imaginary. For instance, there is no record of their going to California with Yellow Serpent's son, and, while Perrin was at The Dalles when the attack at Waiilatpu happened, he did not ride to warn those at Lapwai. That treacherous trip was made by Henry Spalding.

We do know, however, that the Nez Perce liked and trusted Perrin enough to later ask him to be their interpreter in treaty negotiations with the government.

Shikam Pitin is not the real name of Chief Tuekakas's oldest daughter. She was baptized as Celia, and after that her Indian name was lost.

DAVE AND NETA JACKSON are a husband/wife writing team who have authored or coauthored many books on marriage and family, the church, and relationships, including the books accompanying the Secret Adventures video series, the Pet Parables series, and the Caring Parent series.

They have three children: Julian, the illustrator for the Trailblazer series, Rachel, a college student, and Samantha, their high school Cambodian foster daughter. They make their home in Evanston, Illinois, where they are active members of Reba Place Church.

CONTENTS

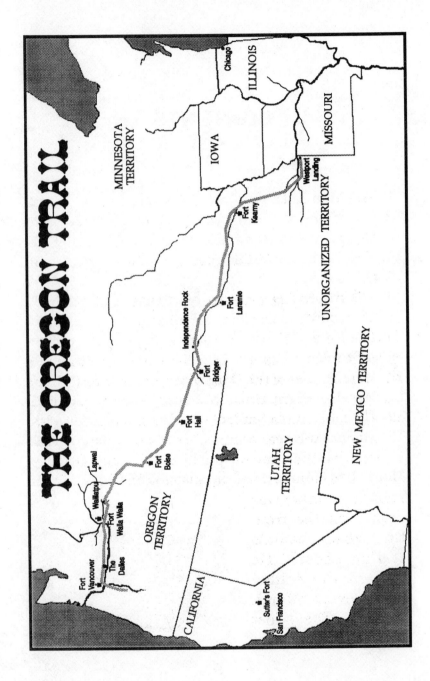

Chapter 1

The Man in the Buffalo Robe

PERRIN WHITMAN RAN into the house and tossed a folded copy of the *Daily Tribune* onto his father's lap. "Is this about Uncle Marcus?" Perrin asked excitedly, brushing a hank of blond hair out of his eyes.

His father's eyes scanned slowly down the article written by the famous publisher Horace Greeley. "Why, I do believe it is," he said slowly. "I didn't even know my brother was back from the fron- tier. What's the date of this paper?" He flipped the folded pages over: "March 29, 1843. That's just last week!"

"He must have traveled cross-country right in the dead of winter," offered Perrin.

"But I don't see how that's possible . . . not from Oregon. From what I've heard, the snows in the mountains can get as deep as the eaves on a house, and in the prairie it drifts something terrible."

"Yeah, and how about Indians?"

Samuel Whitman looked back at the newspaper in his hand. "This says Marcus looks like a ragged mountain man in buckskin clothes with frostbite scars all over his face."

"And look," Perrin added, stepping to the side of his father's chair and pointing to a paragraph in the middle of the article. "He had a meeting with the President of the United States looking like that."

"Yes. Well," the man said, rubbing his hand across his clean-shaven chin, "I've heard that President Tyler is getting more and more interested in the 'Oregon Territory,' as they're calling it now."

"You think Uncle Marcus will come see us, Papa?"

"I should hope so, Son. After all, Rushville is his hometown, even if it's stuck way out here in western New York. But I don't know how we'll entertain him, what with your mother gone and all." Samuel put the paper down, got up from his chair, and walked to the window to hide the tears in his eyes. "She always admired your uncle and hoped you'd be a missionary like him some day."

It had only been a year since Samuel Whitman's wife had died. Since then, it hadn't been easy making a living and keeping house for four children. At almost thirteen, Perrin was the oldest and a good worker, but in the small town of Rushville, there weren't many jobs to keep a growing boy busy. He had to think of the boy's future. . . .

❖ ❖ ❖ ❖

Four days later, when the light of a miserable, drizzly afternoon had almost faded to darkness, Perrin and four friends stood shivering on the porch of the Rushville Mercantile store.

They had almost given up their wait when Perrin announced, "Here it comes."

Sure enough, down the glistening, slippery street rumbled the twice-weekly stagecoach. Steam rolled off the wheezing horses as they were hauled to a stop in front of the town's main store. The stage was so covered with mud that its red paint could only be seen around the top of the coach. The driver jumped down and walked stiffly toward the store with a mail pouch over his arm.

"He ain't coming," whispered one of the boys.

"Hey, mister," called Perrin after the driver, "you got any passengers?"

"Well, there was one feller who climbed in back at Canandaigua. I 'spect he's still there."

The boys stood staring at the coach, still rocking back and forth on its leather suspension straps. Suddenly, the door creaked and swung open. Out backed a huge furry creature that looked like a bear with boots.

Together, the boys stepped back into the shadows of the Mercantile's porch. When the figure, who had been wrestling with a case inside the coach, pulled it free and turned around, the boys saw that it was not a bear but a man—a lean, tall man, made larger than life by the bulk of the great hairy coat that he wore. "That's a buffalo coat," whispered Perrin.

"And he's wearing a fur cap, just like the mountain men," offered one of the other boys.

"That's 'cause he *is* a mountain man, stupid," said Perrin. "I told ya!"

Perrin had not seen his uncle since Marcus Whitman had left to start a mission to the Indians in the wilderness of Oregon seven years before. With him had gone his new wife, the beautiful Narcissa Prentiss; another couple, Henry and Eliza Spalding; and a fifth person, William Gray. Narcissa Whitman and Eliza Spalding had gained great fame in the East because they had been the first white women to cross the continental divide. Before they crossed the Rocky Mountains, the only white families to settle in the West were the few wealthy enough to travel by ship around South America and up the coast to live in coastal cities like Los Angeles or San Francisco.

But seven years is a long time to remember the face of a person you saw last when you were only six years old. Perrin stared hard at the man who stepped up on the porch. The dim light coming out of the store window showed a tall man with a lean, square face and a rough beard. His nose was straight and his eyes were deep set, and there were—as the newspaper article had said—dark frostbite blotches on his cheeks.

"Uncle Marcus?" ventured Perrin.

"Who's that?" rumbled a deep voice as the man turned toward the shadows where the boys were hiding.

"Perrin . . . Perrin Whitman, sir. I came to meet the stage and walk you home."

"You don't say. Well, if you're my true-to-blood nephew, come out here in the light where I can see you."

Perrin stepped forward and shook his uncle's outstretched hand. Then he quickly called his friends forward. They would owe him one if they got to shake hands with a frontiersman as famous as Doctor Marcus Whitman.

The next day was Sunday, and the four boys in front of the store weren't the only people in Rushville who wanted to see Doctor Whitman. The minister arranged for the doctor to speak in church, and nearly the whole town attended, filling all the pews and standing around the back.

As usual, the flue for the wood stove wasn't working properly, and the sunlight shining through the tall windows along the south side of the sanctuary cut bright angling paths through the smoky atmosphere of the small church. Once the congregation had sung all four verses to five hymns—all of them about missions—the wheezing sound of the pedal-pumped organ came to a halt, and the minister stood to announce the speaker: Doctor Marcus Whitman,

Rushville's own missionary to the far reaches of the western wilderness.

Uncle Marcus stepped up to the pulpit. Even though Perrin's father had offered to loan Uncle Marcus a black suit for Sunday "so you won't offend anyone," the frontiersman had dressed in his buckskins. "They're a lot more comfortable than store-bought clothes," he had told Perrin, "even though I'll admit they smell a might strong after wearing 'em for six months."

Perrin, who usually sat with his friends in the back row in church, had his buddies with him in the front row to hear his uncle.

"We have very little time to convert the Indians of the Northwest to Christianity," Doctor Whitman began. "Just twelve short years ago, four brave Nez Perce Indians traveled on their own over twelve hundred miles from the Oregon Territory all the way down to St. Louis. Did they come to trade beaver pelts? No. Did they come to buy liquor? No. They came to ask for THIS!" Marcus shouted, holding his battered black Bible high above his head.

"They wanted Bibles and someone to come and explain the Gospel to them. Can you imagine that, brothers and sisters? People asking for missionaries to come and tell them how to know God! How will we ever answer our Lord in heaven concerning His command to preach the Gospel if we do not at least go to people who are asking to hear?

"I, myself, received such a call. Four years later Reverend Parker and I attended the trappers' rendezvous on the eastern slopes of the Rocky Mountains. Along with all the wild trappers of the Northwest, nearly two thousand Indians were gathered there. On the very day that I arrived, I operated on a famous mountain man named Jim Bridger and removed a three-inch, barbed arrowhead that had been lodged in his back for three years. Many Indians watched and were amazed by Bridger's recovery. After that I was constantly busy doctoring trappers and Indians alike.

"A few days later, at a conference with the chiefs, Reverend Parker explained why we had come: We were exploring the possibility of starting a mission among the Nez Perce Indians in answer to their request.

"Now, brothers and sisters, I want you to listen closely to what the Indians said. The head chief stood up and said, 'We have heard of the coming of a teacher from the Almighty in the company of a remarkable medical man. That is why we came to this rendezvous. I have been told something of the worship of God, but that is all. But if a teacher will come among us, I and my children will obey all that he says.'

"Can you believe that, brothers and sisters? What faith, what openness, what an invitation!" Doctor Whitman shouted as he reached in the air with both arms like he was welcoming the whole world. Then in a quiet, worried voice, he continued, "But we are in danger of losing our opportunity with the Indians. The day of the noble savage who can ride wild and free across the land is nearly gone. If the Indian does not accept the ways of the white man, he will be wiped out. You have seen it here in the East, and it will soon happen in the West. Civilization—our civilization, that is—is spreading. White men bring whiskey and rum and barbed wire, and we kill the game.

"I am committed not only to sharing the Gospel with the Indians but to preparing them so they can survive the advancement of civilization. Indians on our mission station are not only being converted and baptized, but they are learning how to farm and raise cattle. We're getting them ready to endure the arrival of the white man.

"But we need reinforcements. We need *your* help!" he urged.

Perrin heard very little of the rest of what his uncle said. His mind was spinning with visions of high mountains and wild Indians riding like the wind through the sage brush. He wanted to be a part of that adventure. He wanted to go west!

That afternoon around the dinner table, his uncle explained more about why he had come back east. The Presbyterian mission board had threatened to shut the Waiilatpu mission down at just the time Marcus felt it should be expanded.

"The settlers are starting to come," he said urgently. "When Narcissa and I went west, no one thought a family could cross the Rockies. Last year eighteen wagons with over a hundred people pulled into our mission station. Half of them were sick and nearly starved, but there they were, in Oregon. And

I was glad to see them."

"But this morning," said Perrin's father, "I thought you said the arrival of settlers was going to destroy the Indians. How can you be glad to see them?"

"For this reason," explained the missionary. "Great Britain wants to lay claim to the Oregon Territory, and the Hudson's Bay Company has been there for years with its forts and fur traders. Why, Lord Ashburton is down in Washington right now trying to negotiate a treaty to get Oregon for England. That's why I went to see the President. We can't let England have Oregon!"

"But what good will settlers do?" asked Samuel Whitman.

"Settlers are America's claim on Oregon. If we have enough United States citizens in the area, the government will never surrender it to England. If we don't, then the British and their Hudson's Bay Company will take over.

"What I want is the right kind of people to come to Oregon. I've been trying to get the Presbyterian mission board to send funds for founding more schools. I want good people to come as missionary settlers and teachers and helpers."

Perrin saw his chance. "I'll go, Uncle Marcus," he said eagerly.

"What we need are . . ." Marcus stopped in midsentence and looked at young Perrin. He turned nervously to Perrin's father and slowly continued. "What we need are people who care more for the

18

Indians' souls than their land."

"That's me," said Perrin, again trying to edge his way into the conversation. "I don't want any land, but I could help around the mission. There's a lot of things I can do. Isn't that right, Papa? It'd be one less mouth to feed . . . and Lucy could help take care of the younger kids."

There was an awkward silence as the Whitman brothers looked at each other. Finally, Perrin's father said, "I suppose I could get along without you . . . for a while. But I don't think Marcus had young lads in mind when he called for helpers."

"Now hold on there, Samuel," said Marcus. "The frontier makes a man out of a boy pretty fast, and Perrin, here, seems to have gotten a pretty good start. I wouldn't mind taking him with me . . . if you could let him go."

"Oh, please, Papa, please!"

"But . . . would he be safe?" asked Perrin's father, slowly taking the boy's request seriously.

"Well, nothing's really safe on the frontier," Marcus admitted. "There's always the possibility of an accident or something."

"I mean the Indians," said Samuel. "They're savages, aren't they?"

"Well, yes. By our standards they may be savages. They live wildly, by hunting and riding horses. Samuel, I have never in my life seen better horsemen than the Nez Perce. You should see them—"

"That's not what I mean," interrupted Perrin's father.

"No. I suppose it's not. But what can I say, Samuel? They're family people; they're a peace-loving people. But they're being pushed by the white man, and sometimes . . . sometimes there's tension. But do you know what our mission is called? *Waiilatpu*. In Nez Perce, that means the place of the rye grass. There's not a more beautiful, peaceful valley in the whole Northwest. Perrin will be fine."

"I suppose it might do him some good," said Samuel thoughtfully. He turned to his eager son. "But mind you, now, I want no complaining when the going gets rough."

Perrin could hardly believe it. His father was saying yes! He was going to Oregon!

Chapter 2

Dirt Clods at Waiilatpu

THE BRIGHT GREEN RYE GRASS waved gently as the late summer breezes passed through the high mountain valley where the Whitman mission was located. But today Shikam was not in the mission school. At age twelve and the oldest daughter of Chief Tuekakas, she sometimes had to do the chores her younger brother Joseph would someday do.

The Nez Perce girl rode her pony slowly along a meandering creek, looking for horses that had strayed from her father's herd. Her full name, *Shikam Pitin*, meant "Horse Girl," and her father had taught her to ride well. He also

depended on her to help handle his large herd of fine horses. Her reflection in the cool, clear water beside her—slim and straight on the back of her pinto—suddenly rippled as a trout darted from the shadow of a rock to a sunken log, looking for foolish crickets that might have jumped the wrong way off the willow bushes along the bank.

Shikam's hunt for the horses brought her within sight of the Waiilatpu mission station. Along with a blacksmith shop and guest house, the mission included the large T-shaped building that served as combination living quarters for the Whitmans and school for Indian children. Shikam enjoyed school, especially the songs Narcissa Whitman taught the children. She was also learning English and doing quite well . . . but she missed her other school at Lapwai, where her family lived part of the time. At Lapwai, the Spaldings—the other missionary family who had come west with the Whitmans—had been translating Bible stories into the Nez Perce language. It was so much easier for Shikam to understand the stories when they were in her own language.

All of Shikam's family had been baptized as Christians. Sometimes they lived in the Cayuse village near the Whitman mission. Sometimes they lived with the Nez Perce people in Lapwai, the mission of Henry and Eliza Spalding. Her father, Chief Tuekakas, was half Nez Perce and half Cayuse—two closely related Indian tribes.

Shikam's father was respected in the villages of

both tribes, but the chief leader of the Cayuse Indians camped at Waiilatpu was a quarrelsome man called Chief Tilaukait. Shikam did not like him.

This morning, when Shikam did not find any horses along the creek, she galloped across the meadow toward a grove of cottonwood trees near the gristmill at the edge of the Walla Walla River. She had just slowed her horse to a walk when

she heard a loud moan. No one seemed to be at the gristmill grinding flour, so the girl slipped from the back of her pony and cautiously peeked around the corner of the mill. There, sitting on the ground with his back to the wooden building, was the son of Chief Tilaukait. Shikam was about to turn away when the boy leaned forward and vomited miserably. He seemed to be very sick. Shikam moved closer; the mess on the ground was a pale, sickly green. Repulsed, she wanted to back away and leave him alone, but the boy stretched a hand out to her in a pitiful way.

"Tummy-sick . . . evil spirit . . . very bad," he moaned.

It was obvious that the boy needed help. Shikam brought her pony around and helped him crawl up onto it, then she climbed up behind and rode slowly to the Cayuse village, taking care not to ride through the mission garden patches along the river. William Gray, the man who was helping Narcissa Whitman while her husband was gone to the East, always yelled at the Indians if they went through the garden.

When she arrived in the village, Shikam discovered that several other people were tummy-sick, and all of them seemed to be throwing up the same green liquid. As she helped the boy off her pony beside his father's lodge, several of the headmen were standing outside talking in angry voices. Her own father was there, though he seemed to be silent.

"The whites have put a curse on us. Everyone is sick," shouted Chief Tilaukait. "We should chase them away while Doctor Whitman is gone!"

"Chasing them away won't help," snorted Tomahas, another bad-tempered man that Shikam didn't like. "If we chase them away, they will just come back, and more with them. We should kill them; then others will be afraid to come to Waiilatpu."

"We must do something," Chief Tilaukait said. "The whites are getting stronger. Today they make us tummy-sick. Tomorrow, we may die from their bad medicine."

Finally, Shikam's father spoke up. "Tummy-sick Indians only throw up melons. Why is that?"

"The whites put a curse on their melons. That's why," spat Tomahas.

Chief Tuekakas continued his patient reasoning. "I have eaten their melon and did not get sick, but it was a melon they gave my daughter, Shikam, when she was at the mission school."

Shikam slid around behind her pony, so she would not be noticed by the men. Her father continued, "Could it be the melons that make people sick have been stolen and not given to us?"

"Stolen!" shouted Chief Tilaukait. "How can an Indian steal the fruit of his own earth? This whole valley belongs to us. Anything that grows from it we can eat."

"Even that which you did not plant?" pressed Chief Tuekakas.

"You are too friendly with the whites," Chief Tilaukait said angrily. "You have accepted their God.

Maybe He protects you from the white man's curse."

"Maybe so, maybe not. I would not know because I have not eaten any stolen melons. But if you think the whites have put a curse on you, why don't you face them with your accusations?"

"We will do that," said Chief Tilaukait. "We will see what they have to say." He slung his blanket around his shoulder in an angry gesture and marched off toward the Whitman mission.

"*Then* we should kill them," muttered Tomahas as he and the other men followed along.

A chill went up Shikam's back. Tomahas's name meant "murderer," and she had the feeling he just might live up to his name someday. Tuekakas and other Indians joined the little delegation as they walked through the village. Leaving her pony, Shikam followed along behind. A bony dog, thinking he was being chased, tucked his tail between his legs and scampered off in a little cloud of dust.

The group of Indians crossed the field and entered the yard of the mission house. But instead of calling for Mrs. Whitman to come out and talk, which was the polite thing to do when approaching someone's lodge, Chief Tilaukait threw the door open and barged in. Shikam could hear Mrs. Whitman yelling and some of the schoolchildren screaming. Pretty soon, William Gray succeeded in pushing Chief Tilaukait out the door.

It was not a battle of strength or Chief Tilaukait would have remained inside, because he was much stronger than William Gray. Shikam knew he had barged in as an insult, not because that was where he wanted to talk.

In a moment, a flushed Mrs. Whitman appeared on the steps of the house. She was an attractive woman—or would be, if she'd let her hair out of the severe bun she wore. "What do you want?" she asked, trying to sound angry, but Shikam could hear the fear in her voice.

"Why have you put a curse on us?" shouted Chief Tilaukait. "Our people are tummy-sick."

"Sick? Why, it's probably just a summer flu . . . or maybe you've eaten something bad. If my husband were here, he could give you medicine to soothe your stomachs, but he's still back east. I'm sorry; you'll just have to make do. Now, please go back home. I'm trying to teach school."

"The only bad thing we've eaten is melon," accused Tomahas.

"Melons?" said Narcissa Whitman with genuine surprise. "The only melons around here are mission melons. How did you get melons?"

The door behind Mrs. Whitman opened. "They stole them," announced William Gray as he stepped out to stand behind the missionary woman. Shikam could see the round faces of some of the schoolchildren through the windows. For some reason, she wished she were inside with them this morning.

"You have cursed the melons," accused Chief Tilaukait.

"The melons aren't cursed," said William Gray, stepping around Narcissa Whitman to face the angry mob. "I simply put a little poison on them to teach you thieving savages a lesson."

An angry murmur went through the band of Indians gathered in the yard. But Narcissa Whitman cried out, "Mr. Gray! Such an action is unforgivable! I cannot believe it of you."

"It's not going to harm anyone," Gray said defensively. "It's just going to upset their stomachs. Maybe they throw up a little; so what? It serves 'em right."

"But why? We are here to help these people, not make them sick."

"The problem is," Mr. Gray said, his voice rising, "they've been helping themselves from *my* melon patch! I've chased them off time and again, and I've warned them to quit stealing my melons. Finally, I got tired of it and decided to teach 'em a lesson."

"So you *poisoned* them? Is that the Christian way?" Mrs. Whitman was clearly upset.

"I didn't poison the Indians—just the melons," sneered Gray. "You can be sure the only savages who are sick are the thieves!"

Narcissa Whitman stood in the yard, hands on her hips. "Mr. Gray, I will not stand for this. I want you out of Waiilatpu by sundown. Go up to Lapwai with the Spaldings if you want to, but don't set foot on this mission station again until my husband returns and can deal with you!"

Gray's eyes shifted uneasily. "Mrs. Whitman, I would gladly be rid of you and these Cayuse savages, but without a white man on the station, you would not be safe."

"Get out! Get out now! If I am in any danger, it is the danger you have brought on us all. Now be gone."

Shikam blinked. She had never seen white people so angry—certainly not toward one another.

"You leave, too," shouted Chief Tilaukait to Mrs. Whitman. "We do not want any white people here. We do not need the mission. This is our land."

"I will not leave until my husband returns," said Narcissa. Then, bursting into tears, she pushed her way past William Gray and back into the house, slamming the door. Shikam heard the wooden bar fall in place across the door, locking William Gray outside.

Suddenly a clod of dirt hit the side of the mission house not a foot away from Gray's head. Then another found its mark in the middle of his chest. Seeing how angry the crowd had become, he ran around the side of the building and raced to the stable where he normally slept. A few Indian boys followed, hurrying him along with more dirt clods.

Shikam fell in beside her father as they walked back to the Cayuse village. "Will the white people really leave?" she asked.

"I do not know, my daughter. I think their God is good, even though some of them are bad. But the Whitmans—though sometimes ignorant—have a good heart."

Shikam sighed. "I hope Mrs. Whitman doesn't leave. I like going to school."

Chapter 3

Doctorin' and Ramroddin'

PERRIN WHITMAN STOOD by his uncle on the upper deck of the riverboat as it paddled up the Missouri River. "Are all these people going to Oregon?" he asked, amazed at all the men, women, and children packed on the boat. It was the last day of May 1843.

"It seems so," said Marcus Whitman. "Everyone is headed to Westport to join the new wagon train. This is exactly what I said would happen when I spoke with the President of the United States, but I had no idea it would be happening so soon. People are moving west, and that's the way Oregon is going to be saved for the United States."

"Who is it being saved from . . . the Indians?"

"No-o, no . . . saved from the British, lad. The Hudson's Bay Company has filled the Northwest with British trappers to the point that American fur men have all but disappeared. They were sure the whole territory was going British. But now . . . now come the American settlers—to stay. They will save the day."

"But what about the Indians?" Perrin persisted.

"Well, like I told your papa, their only hope is to adapt to the white man's ways, and the best way to adapt is through the civilizing power of Christianity. But . . . the Presbyterian mission board won't send more missionaries to help us do the job. So, maybe the settlers will be a substitute. Most are Christians—at least they claim to be."

"But the settlers aren't going out to Oregon to be missionaries. They're after land, aren't they? And that land belongs to the Indians, doesn't it?"

Marcus Whitman frowned. "That's a problem, to be sure. But there's lots of land, more than you can ever imagine. If the settlers behave themselves like Christians, and if the Indians are willing to change their ways—learn to farm and obey laws—then everything should work out."

"But it didn't work out in the East, did it? Most Indians were run off or killed, from what I've heard."

"You do ask the most troublesome questions, Perrin," said Marcus Whitman with a short laugh. "There. Look ahead, around that bend in the river. I think that's Westport. But, wha—? Looks like the whole place is on fire."

A thick cloud hung above the little town. It was either smoke or dust or both, and the setting sun blazed a deep red through it.

The steamboat whistle let out such a piercing blast that Perrin instinctively ducked; then the splashing throb of the stern paddlewheel slowed its speed as the boat worked its way up to the bank to discharge its many passengers and all their gear.

Perrin and his uncle grabbed their large packs and were some of the first people down the plank onto the crowded riverbank. "I never imagined Westport like this," said Marcus, winding his way through the piles of supplies stacked in every available space. The town was nothing more than a few clapboard buildings arranged along its one and only "main street," but it was as busy as a small city. "Whoever thought so many people would be going west!"

Built up around the town was a tent and wagon city. Some of the temporary shelters were set up in a haphazard fashion, while others stood in an orderly arrangement extending the streets of the town, or circled, ready to move out. It did not take the boy and his uncle long to see that the cloud hanging over the town was created by a mixture of dust churned up by the constantly moving teams of oxen and mules and smoke from the campfires of the pioneers.

"Hmm. We might have a problem," said Uncle Marcus, surveying the crowded main street. "I had expected to buy us a couple horses or mules here, but I've got a feeling that there won't be many for sale."

That night the two Whitmans slept on the outskirts of the camp, propped up against their packs with Marcus's great buffalo coat over them both. Early next morning as Marcus set off to look for a couple horses, he said, "Mark my words, boy. A couple weeks down the trail, these people will be throwing so much stuff away you'll have to duck to keep from getting hit. But right now, they're grabbin' everything in sight they think might be useful in Oregon. So you stay here and keep an eye on our gear, okay? Likely as not someone will try to steal it."

Perrin scowled. "Steal? These are the same 'Christian' people you hope will treat the Indians fairly when it comes to land?"

"You just watch our gear," said Doctor Whitman. He knew Perrin's question wasn't a true question but a smart remark sparked by disappointment at having to stand guard.

By ten o'clock, Perrin saw that teams of oxen or mules had been hitched to most of the wagons, and they'd started to pull out, leaving behind still-smoldering cooking fires and so much trash that the area looked like a battlefield. Still, Uncle Marcus had not returned with horses for them to ride.

Suddenly, Perrin heard a scream from one of the wagons. "Stop, stop! The baby, the baby!" cried a terrified woman. Perrin ran across the dusty lot in time to see that a toddler had fallen under the wheel of a heavy wagon. The child was alive, but seriously hurt.

Uncle Marcus—he is a doctor! Perrin thought. The boy did not wait to learn more but took off running. Perrin was completely out of breath when he finally found his uncle down by the river trying to buy a broken-down donkey from an old trapper.

"You keep that donkey for me," Whitman told the trapper as he ran off with his nephew. "I'll be back for him later."

"Can't make no promises," called the old-timer.

Doctor Whitman worked with the injured child for most of the day, but in the late afternoon, the toddler gave a last rasping breath and died. Perrin felt terrible. The family hadn't even gotten out of town before tragedy struck. And they'd looked so well prepared and hopeful. Their wagon was a new one and well built. Besides the six muscular oxen pulling the wagon, they had four large horses, a milk cow, and a dozen cattle. Everything looked in good shape . . . except for the woman. She did not look strong. There were four other children, all under the age of seven, and though they were well dressed, they, too, looked thin and weak.

"We got to dig a grave and bury little Joseph," said the father huskily.

"Not 'til tomorrow," declared the woman. Her eyes were bright and stubborn through her tears.

"But we've got to get movin'," her husband said

desperately. "Most of the wagon train has several hours head start on us. We gotta catch up."

It was true. All that afternoon, wagons had been pulling out, until this was the last one left.

"I ain't goin'," said the woman.

"I know how ya feel, Mother. But we must; there's no other choice!"

"Yes, there is. I'm not goin' to Oregon."

"You're what?"

"I said, I'm not going to Oregon! Simple as that."

Perrin felt awkward and embarrassed listening to the couple argue. But he waited as his uncle repacked his doctor's kit.

"But what are we going to do?" asked her husband. "We sold our place in Ohio; we can't go back."

"We'll stay here!"

"Here? And do what?" asked the man.

"We can buy a little place and farm . . . or, or maybe set up a store to supply future emigrants. But I'm not moving on and leavin' my youngun behind in the ground!"

The man tugged on his hat, looking sad but exasperated. "You're from Oregon, Doctor Whitman. Do ya think there's going to be another emigrant train?"

Whitman shook his head. "Not this year. Anyone who doesn't get on the trail within the next few days will be too late to make it over the mountains before winter. But take heart, man . . . with so many people going out this year, there's bound to be more next year. You see, when these people start writing letters home and telling about the paradise they've found . . . well, this is just the beginning."

Doctor Whitman and Perrin finally left the bereaved family and again went looking for horses or mules to ride to Oregon. The old trapper with the donkey had gotten on a steamboat and headed downriver, and in the entire town there didn't seem to be an extra horse or mule.

It was dark before they gave up looking and walked over to the hotel. "Looks like we're goin' to have to walk," said Marcus, lowering his big bulk into a wooden chair on the hotel porch. He tugged off his left boot and began to rub his foot. "Don't know if this bum foot o' mine can make it. But . . . guess I'll never know until we try, right, boy? Let's see if we can get some sleep."

The two Whitmans had no trouble getting a room in Westport's little six-room hotel that night; the town was nearly empty. Before they went to sleep in the creaky bed, Perrin wondered out loud, "Uncle Marcus, if we can't catch the wagon train, will we have to walk to Oregon alone?"

Marcus chuckled. "The wagon train won't travel far the first few days. Might take us a week or so, but we'll still catch 'em, even on foot."

In the morning the two travelers headed off carrying their heavy packs. "We might end up dumping some of this gear ourselves if we have to carry our packs all the way," Marcus laughed.

On the edge of town they passed the wagon of pioneers who had lost the baby. The family was preparing to bury the small body, so Marcus and

Perrin stopped and joined the grieving family at the graveside. When the simple service was over and they had picked up their packs, the father cleared his throat. "Uh—Doctor Whitman, I appreciate your efforts tryin' to save my baby. An' seein' as how we won't be movin' on—at least not this year—I'd be glad to sell you a couple horses, if you want."

Within thirty minutes the doctor and his nephew had two fine bay horses under saddle and were off down the trail. "Wa-hoo!" shouted Perrin. In three hours of easy riding, they had caught up with the slow-moving wagon train.

❖ ❖ ❖ ❖

The wagon train was the biggest of its kind that had ever headed across country. Over one thousand men, women, and children were traveling in 120 wagons drawn by teams of oxen or mules, and herding nearly five thousand horses and cattle—not counting miscellaneous dogs, cats, and chickens. The wagons bulged with heavy furniture, and most pioneers were inexperienced in handling the bulky contraptions up and down riverbanks and across rivers.

Once the caravan got going each day, it stretched for miles. Doctor Whitman and Perrin rode up and down the column offering medical aid and practical help wherever they were needed. There was always someone sick to be treated or a wagon wheel to be repaired. In exchange for their help, they were often invited to have a meal around an evening campfire.

They had been on the trail less than two weeks when Perrin saw his first wild Indians. From out of the seemingly flat prairie, ninety Kansas and Osage warriors suddenly emerged on prancing ponies. The Indians had lances, shields, bows and arrows, and their faces were painted red. Feathers hung from their black hair. They raced up and down the column of wagons, sometimes swerving close, as though they were going to attack.

Meanwhile, the leaders of the wagon train were yelling for the wagons to circle for defense, but the men were too busy getting their guns ready and trying to aim at the Indians.

The Indians' wild yells spooked some of the pioneers' horses, which bolted away from the wagon train. Suddenly, the warriors altered their circling route around the wagon train and galloped after the straying horses. Quickly they herded the strays together and disappeared over a small rise.

"Boy, that was close!" said Perrin, wide-eyed.

"They didn't intend to harm us," said Marcus with a chuckle. "They were just collecting their toll payment from us for crossing their land."

"Toll payment?"

"Yeah . . . like when you pay a toll to ride a ferry across a river? Well, they just charged us to cross their land."

"But nobody paid them money," said Perrin, not understanding.

"Maybe not in gold, but those horses were worth a good deal. I'd say it was a rather high toll, myself."

That night the leaders decided to break the wagon train into two groups. It would be easier to circle the wagons in times of danger, and possibly the smaller numbers would be less threatening to the Indians. But the groups would remain close enough so that if one were attacked, help could come from the other.

During the days that followed, other Indians approached the wagon trains. Sometimes they came peacefully; sometimes they behaved threateningly. Usually, they stole a little food or a few horses or made it obvious that they did not like the whites crossing their land, but there was never a serious attack.

Days stretched into weeks. Often Marcus Whitman proved more useful as a guide than John Gantt, who had been hired for the job. Marcus was good at selecting a river crossing, or suggesting the quickest detour around mountains, or finding a "nooning" site of water and grass for a short rest in the middle of the day.

Always, Marcus hurried the settlers on to Oregon. His goal was for the wagon train to reach Independence Rock by the Fourth of July. Otherwise, they would be in danger of getting caught in the snows before they got over the mountains. "Travel, *travel*, TRAVEL—nothing else will take you to the end of the journey; nothing is wise that does not help you along; nothing is good for you that causes a moment's delay," urged Whitman.

Whitman's ramroddin' had pushed the wagon trains across the prairie with remarkable success,

and on the morning of July second, as some low-lying clouds cleared away, the travelers saw the unmistakable crown of Independence Rock in the distance. They were going to make it, possibly a day ahead of schedule!

Perrin galloped ahead with a few others to select the best place to camp. They kept up a fast pace all day and arrived at the base of Independence Rock by midafternoon. There, near the Sweetwater River that meandered through the beautiful valley at the base of the important landmark, they found a camp of some fur traders headed east. The traders had a mail pouch with them, and when they discovered that Perrin was the nephew of Doctor Whitman, they gave him a letter to deliver to his uncle.

Before sunset, Perrin climbed the rugged bluff of Independence Rock and scratched his name into the stone alongside many others: "Perrin Whitman, 1843. For Oregon."

The next day, Perrin rode back toward the wagon train and delivered the letter to his uncle. But after reading it, the doctor was silent. When Perrin asked what it said, Marcus just handed it to him.

Dear Husband,

William Gray nearly started an uprising among the Indians by poisoning melons to punish them for stealing. I sent him packing. Also, someone is circulating rumors that you went east to recruit soldiers to come back and destroy them all. Of course, they are very upset.

There has been trouble at the mission at Lapwai, too.

Do you remember Elijah White? He served with the Methodist missionaries until they sent

him home for stirring up so much trouble.
Well, he's back. This time he's claiming to have
authority as the United States Government's
Indian agent, and he wants to have a pow-wow
with the Indians to set up some laws. In my
opinion, he will do far more harm than good. I
wish he would just go back east.

Last week I was awakened by someone raising the latch on the door to my room. I jumped
up and tried to close the door again, but he was
much stronger than I. It was one of the Indians—possibly Chief Tilaukait himself, but I
can't be sure. I screamed and screamed until
he finally left.

Somehow Mr. McKenlay from Fort Walla
Walla heard about what happened, and this
morning he came to get me. I didn't want to
abandon our mission in Waiilatpu, but he insisted and has brought me here to the Methodist mission at The Dalles. I must admit that I
am grateful to be safe. I may go on down to
Fort Vancouver until you return.

I wish you were here.

Love,
Narcissa

Chapter 4

Fire in the Gristmill

T HE NIGHT AFTER NARCISSA WHITMAN LEFT Waiilatpu, Shikam was boiling some camas roots in a water-tight basket by the fire. Each heated rock sizzled wildly as she dropped it into the pot to bring the water to a boil. Shikam turned her head away from the rising steam and looked off through the Indian camp into the darkness.

She blinked her eyes, thinking for an instant that another puff of steam had floated up reflecting the glow of the fire beside her. But it was not steam. The flickering light she saw was coming from somewhere across the little valley near the Walla Walla River. She stood up and stared into the night until she realized what it was: fire.

"Father, come quickly!" she called.

Chief Tuekakas swung open the flap of their tepee and stepped out.

"Look," Shikam said and pointed into the darkness.

"It's the gristmill," he said grimly. Grabbing several baskets, he called loudly for others in the village to help fight the fire, then he took off at a run. Several of the Cayuse joined him, but others just stood with their arms folded across their chests and watched the flames leap higher into the purple sky.

Shikam ran with the fire fighters across the meadow toward the burning gristmill. When they arrived, there were already other Indians there, but they weren't fighting the fire. They were just standing back, watching. Chief Tuekakas and those who had come with him began scooping baskets of water from the river and throwing them on the building. Shikam joined in, but it was obviously a lost cause. The fire was so hot that they couldn't get close enough for the water to reach the hottest parts of the blaze.

"Why do you try to save the white man's mill?" called a voice from the shadows. It was Tomahas.

"Why not?" grunted Tuekakas as he threw water toward the blaze. "I would fight fire even if it were burning your worthless lodge."

"You are stupid to fight the fire. It is too late."

Then Tomahas yelled to the five or six young men with him and ran off into the night toward the mission.

In a last halfhearted effort, the fire fighters threw two or three more baskets of water on the fire, and then stopped. Tomahas was right; there was no hope of saving the mill.

✧ ✧ ✧

The next morning Shikam rode her pony across the meadow to the old mill. She wanted to see the damage by daylight. But even though she had seen the fire last night, she was shocked by the blackened ruins. Even the bags of grain that had been stored inside were worthless. She turned away. Fire could be a friend—cooking food or warming the tepee at night—but it was a fierce enemy when burning out of control. The mill may have been just a white man's building, but the still-smoking pillars and fallen beams were as grim as a blackened forest. Everything looked different; everything was ugly.

As the Indian girl led her pony through the rye grass with a sad heart, she wandered toward the mission. She knew it would be a sad place without Mrs. Whitman there, but she missed school and wanted to see it again.

But when she got to the mission house and school, she was shocked to discover that the windows of the T-shaped building were all broken out and the door was torn partially off its hinges.

Shikam approached the building cautiously. "Hello!" she called. "Is someone here?" But she heard no sound in the still morning. She hesitated on the steps but finally crept in. The furniture was turned over and broken. Doctor Whitman's desk was up-ended, and his papers scattered about the room. The chest of medicines had also been smashed. The room looked like a huge bear had broken into the building and gone crazy ripping everything open looking for juicy black ants to eat.

Shikam froze. There was a noise coming from the kitchen . . . a soft metal sound—*clink, clink, clink*—in a steady rhythm. The girl resisted the urge to flee and slowly crept across the chaotic room. The door to the kitchen stood half open, but she still couldn't see what was making the noise. She took a step more and slowly pushed the door open.

Suddenly, there was a wild screech, and something raced past her and out the front door. Her heart pounding wildly, Shikam realized that it was only one of the half-wild cats that lived around the mission. It had been up on the table licking cream from the large pan used for separating milk from the cream.

When she got back to the village, Shikam told her father about the wrecked mission building. A frown clouded his face. "Very bad medicine," he said. "Bad medicine here. This village is not a good place to live." He turned to Arenoth, his Cayuse wife. "We will leave in the morning."

"But where will we go?" asked Arenoth, pulling

Shikam's younger brother and sister closer to her. "The Cayuse are my people."

"We will go to Lapwai. The Nez Perce people there are also our people. And there are missionaries there to teach us more about God's Son . . . the One they call Jesus."

✧ ✧ ✧ ✧

When Chief Tuekakas and his family arrived at Lapwai three days later, pulling their tepee and other belongings on a *travois* behind their ponies, they discovered that there had been trouble there, too. Some of the non-Christian Nez Perce Indians had been tormenting Eliza Spalding with threats and nasty comments outside her schoolhouse. Also, one angry Indian had held a cocked gun against Henry Spalding's chest for three or four minutes. But the brave missionary brushed the episodes aside. "Isolated incidents, Chief Tuekakas," he assured Shikam's father. "I don't think these acts represent any ill will from most of the Nez Perce."

But the incidents troubled Chief Tuekakas. "I don't like it," he said to his family as they sat around their first campfire in the Lapwai village. "Trouble spreads too fast when it flies on the wings of rumors."

"What rumors, Father?" asked Shikam, sucking on the smoked fish her mother had prepared for supper.

"A rumor that Doctor Whitman went to get soldiers to take away our land from us. Such a rumor would make anyone angry."

"But . . . it isn't true, is it, Father?"

"No, noble daughter. I do not believe it is true. However, Spalding says a government man is coming by the name of Elijah White. This man claims to speak for the great white chief from the rising of the sun—the 'President,' as Doctor Whitman calls him. I do not like it, but we are supposed to have a council with this man in three days."

The next few days were busy as delegation after delegation of Indians arrived at the Lapwai camp. In all, twenty-two mighty chiefs arrived with their families and supporting Indians. Chief Tuekakas was recognized as a chief among the Cayuse as well as the Nez Perce, but the only other Cayuse chief to attend was Tuekakas's half brother, Chief Five Crows.

On the morning of the first council day, Chief Tuekakas dressed in his ceremonial clothes, soft buckskins beautifully decorated with beadwork. Shikam helped him put on his large headdress made of eagle feathers. Then her father climbed onto his glossy black mustang, a well-muscled horse that had won many races. Shikam, her mother, sister, and little brother Joseph were also dressed in their finest clothes. Shikam's white buckskin tunic was decorated with hundreds of bright red beads, and she wove strips of bright red cloth into her hair.

All the other chiefs were also dressed in their finest ceremonial clothes.

On one side of a large field was the tent of Elijah White and the six men with him. They were standing out in front along with the missionaries from Lapwai, Henry and Eliza Spalding. On the other side of the field the Indian chiefs assembled on their best horses. Shikam was proud of her people. She knew that the Nez Perce were the finest horse breeders and trainers in the Northwest. Horses were the primary sign of wealth among the tribes. Many families owned seventy or eighty horses, and some of the great chiefs owned several hundred.

When the signal was given, they turned as one and galloped at top speed around the open meadow, racing past the observing white men. Then the Indians withdrew to the far side of the meadow, wheeled and charged in a column four abreast toward Elijah White and his men. They fired their guns into the air, beat their drums, and blew on their war whistles. At the last instant, the column split, two riders of each wave going to the right and two to the left. They were so close to White before they turned that dust and even foam from the horses' mouths spattered the faces of the white men. It was a tremendous demonstration of horsemanship and fighting skill.

Elijah White bravely stood his ground, and then clapped and saluted the Indians when on a final signal they positioned themselves in a semicircle in front of him. After the demonstration, the council meeting began.

Shikam squeezed her way to the front of the crowd that surrounded the chiefs and the white men; she wanted to hear everything that was said. Mr. White started by saying that the government had sent him to protect the Indians. Shikam didn't see why her people needed protecting; they had always been able to take care of themselves.

Then he said that the missionaries were highly respected by the white people, and that the white people would make sure no harm came to them. "But," he said, "some very bad things have happened lately." He mentioned the violence at Waiilatpu and the threats at Lapwai. "Those must stop! Therefore, I have written these Ten Rules of Conduct that will govern you." And he began to read:

1. Whoever willfully takes life shall be hung.
2. Whoever burns a dwelling house shall be hung.
3. Whoever burns an outbuilding shall be imprisoned.
4. Whoever carelessly burns a house or any property shall pay damages.
5. If anyone enters a dwelling without permission, he shall be punished.
6. If anyone steals, he shall pay back twice the value of what he steals and receive a whipping of fifty lashes.
7. If anyone takes a horse without permission or any object without permission, he shall pay for its use and receive a whipping of twenty to fifty lashes.
8. If anyone enters a field and damages crops or knocks down fences so that horses or cattle damage crops, he shall pay damages and receive a whipping of twenty-five lashes.
9. Only those who travel or live among game animals may keep dogs. But if a dog kills a lamb or calf or any domestic animal, the owner shall pay the damages and kill the dog.
10. If anyone raises a gun or other weapon against another person, he shall be punished.

Mr. White paused as loud murmurs rose among his listeners. Some of the chiefs were nodding in agreement, but others looked very upset. It was obvious that most of the laws involved wrongs done against the missionaries, because the tribes had their own ways of dealing with similar violations between Indians. But Shikam knew the violence against the missionaries had to be stopped somehow.

"Who will give out these punishments?" asked Five Crows calmly.

"If an Indian breaks one of these laws, the chiefs will punish him or answer to me."

"What about when the white man does wrong things?" said Five Crows. He told about William Gray poisoning melons to make the Indians sick.

"Why did he poison them?"

"He did not want the Indians stealing them," admitted Five Crows. "But they were growing out of Indian ground."

"Well, there you have it. It was the Indians' fault in the first place," said White. "But don't you worry. If a white man does something wrong, you tell me, and if it is his fault, he will be punished, too. You chiefs punish Indian violators, and I will punish white violators."

Shikam knew that Chief Tilaukait and Tomahas had used the melon incident to stir up trouble against the missionaries, but she also felt that William Gray had been wrong in poisoning the melons . . . and hadn't Mrs. Whitman ordered him to leave Waiilatpu for doing it? Somehow, Mr. White's response didn't seem completely fair.

The debate was long and difficult, but in the end the chiefs agreed to accept Mr. White's Ten Rules of Conduct. However, as they left the council, Shikam's father said to her, "Five Crows and I were the only Cayuse at this council. We cannot speak for all the other Cayuse chiefs. I am afraid that the Cayuse people may not abide by Mr. White's rules, and that could mean trouble."

❖ ❖ ❖ ❖

A week after Mr. White and his delegation left Lapwai, Shikam's father took her on a walk to the top of a small hill near their camp. Shikam knew such a walk meant that he had something important to discuss with her. As his oldest child, these talks always made her feel important.

"I don't know if you remember Chief Stickus, Shikam. He is from the Cayuse tribe that we fished for salmon with last season. He and some other Indians are going on a trip to meet Doctor Whitman. Doctor Whitman should be coming west at this time of year, probably with more of those dreadful white settlers—which I do not want to see. However, I don't think we can stop them, and they will need fresh supplies and fresh horses. Stickus plans to sell grain and horses to them and get rich.

"I, too, would like to sell some of my horses to them, but I cannot make the trip. I must go to Waiilatpu. There is more trouble there, and I must see what I can do. But if I had a brave daughter, one who knew how to herd horses and could make a long journey, maybe she could go meet Doctor Whitman and the white settlers and sell them horses."

The old chief looked off across the valley in silence as though he were dreaming of a far-off place. Shikam wanted to squeal with excitement and joy, but she remained silent and dignified, waiting for her father to continue.

Finally, he spoke. "Would you know of such a brave one?"

"I am brave, Father, and I have herded horses for you all this past year."

"So you have. But this would be a long, hard trip. There would be many hardships and dangers. You might even meet bears in the mountains."

Shikam did not beg. She just looked steadily out across the valley like her father.

"You will leave in three days," the chief finally said, a slight smile on his lips.

Chapter 5

On to Oregon

EACH DAY AS THE GREAT WAGON TRAIN moved slowly through the Snake River country, Perrin Whitman rode scout with his uncle as they guided the pioneers across the rocky, parched landscape. When the doctor had traveled east through the area the winter before, he had been riding hard to escape the winter snows and had made the grueling four hundred miles from Waiilatpu to Fort Hall in an incredibly short ten days. He hadn't been looking for where wagons could cross a gully or the easiest path around the next butte.

But going west in the late summer of 1843, his

job was to find a trail that nearly starved oxen pulling worn-out wagons could cross. Sometimes Marcus Whitman and Perrin came across the tracks of a previous caravan, but the tracks often quickly disappeared or led to a sheer drop-off into the raging Snake River canyon below. Tracks did not guarantee that the travelers got through without having to turn around and retrace their steps.

Even when Marcus thought he remembered the trail from his journey west seven years earlier, the old trail was often washed away or blocked by great rockslides, and just as often Doctor Whitman was mistaken. Seven years is a long time to remember a path you traveled only once.

The exhausted emigrants were thirsty under the torturous sun. The raging river that snaked along through sharp volcanic rock formations in the bottom of a steep canyon was usually out of reach. The countryside was parched and harsh. The dogs howled because the hot sand blistered their paws, and the children often cried from hunger.

Perrin was amazed that the wagon train had even continued beyond Fort Hall. When the exhausted travelers had arrived at the fort, the British trader in charge expressed great concern for their welfare. "Dear friends," he said, "I'm grateful you made it this far. Many times along the trail you have braved many difficulties and dangers. I know you want to get to Oregon, but . . . *you must not continue.* Even if the road is passable, our supplies are limited, and we do not have enough to see you through to your intended destination. However, if you are wise enough to turn back to civilization, I will do everything I can to help you."

Perrin could tell his uncle was suspicious of this offer to help them return.

"Some of you have already lost close friends and family members along the way," the trader went on. "They were brave people, but they did not understand the risks. Do not add to their tragedy by sacrificing more loved ones. I am telling you plainly, it is impossible to take wagons over the mountains to the west. You will die if you try. I beg you, please don't attempt it!"

"That's a lie!" shouted Marcus Whitman. "It *is* possible to cross the mountains. Three years ago Joe Meek and his companions took some wagons over the mountains, and it can be done again. You, sir, are an agent of the British Government, and that's why you don't want these good people to settle Oregon. Because when they do, it will help Oregon become American territory."

The weary travelers had cheered . . . but the guides who had brought them as far as Fort Hall quit the next day.

After two days of confusion, the emigrants voted to employ Marcus Whitman to take them on to Oregon. "On to Oregon!" became their rallying cry. It was picked up by the haggard mothers and rawboned fathers and the skinny children with months of dust in their hair. "On to Oregon! On to Oregon!" they cried. Some even painted the slogan on the tattered canvas of their wagon tops. They would not give up.

"These are the salt-of-the-earth people who are going to make Oregon a part of the United States," Doctor Whitman boasted to the British trader as the wagon train prepared to pull out of Fort Hall.

"Maybe," conceded the Englishman. "But a lot of people will die before it's over."

"Is that a threat? Is Britain planning to send in the redcoats again?"

"I doubt it," said the man. "I was thinking of the Indians. This will end their way of life."

"Their way of life was over the first time your Hudson's Bay Company traded them a jug of rum for their beaver pelts."

"We don't do that anymore," said the man defensively.

"Maybe not, but the Indians' only hope now is to adapt to the white man's civilization."

"Yes . . . and surrender all their land to these settlers. But, I'm warning you, the Indians won't give up their land without a fight."

"There's plenty of land for everyone," scoffed Whitman. Then with a quick wave, he spurred his horse out the gate of the fort and to the front of the column of wagons.

As Perrin and his uncle rode over the crest of a rocky mountain trail one afternoon, Doctor Whitman pointed ahead. "We're going to make it," he said, excitement edging his tired voice. "See that big pine tree in the valley below? That's Lone Tree. I know exactly where we are!"

The valley looked like the Garden of Eden compared to the parched wilderness through which they'd been traveling. It seemed to beckon, green and inviting, and that night, as the wagon train began to make camp around the great pine tree, everyone felt confident.

Two nights later they made camp along the Grande Ronde River. Doctor Whitman showed the settlers how to recognize the tasty camas root that looked like an onion but turned black when cooked. Some settlers caught salmon. Others shot ducks in the nearby marshes, and there were freshwater clams to be taken from the river. Everyone had plenty to eat that night.

Ahead of them, however, was the long pull up the Blue Mountains, the last range before the mission station, and many of the oxen were so worn out that they were nearly ready to drop. The little grass they had eaten at the last few stops had not restored their strength.

In the afternoon of September twenty-third, Perrin's sharp eyes saw something on the distant mountains. "Uncle Marcus!" he called, galloping to the front of the wagon train. "There's something coming down the mountain."

"Where?" The doctor shaded his eyes against the afternoon sun.

"There. Right below that saddle between those two peaks. See the dust? It looks like a whole line of riders. Do you think it's more trappers going east with their furs?"

The doctor squinted as they rode along. "Now I see 'em. Those wouldn't be trappers coming east this time of year. The snows would catch them this late. I expect it's Indians . . . and a lot of 'em at that."

But soon Perrin could see that there were only a few riders—and a lot of horses. "Don't worry," shouted Marcus Whitman when the Indians were only half a mile away. "They're Cayuse. And that's Chief Stickus. I know him . . . know him well. He's a good man. We're very fortunate."

The Indians and the wagon train met at the bottom of the first real swoop up the Blue Mountains. They all camped together that night among majestic pine trees by a pleasant creek.

Some of the emigrants objected to the high price the Indians charged for their sacks of flour, but most of the settlers were so eager to eat some sourdough biscuits or pancakes that they paid the price without complaint. A few adventurous women even managed to bake small loaves of bread in their Dutch ovens.

The next morning was spent in serious trading. The Indians offered fresh horses in exchange for the bony cattle and oxen of the settlers. Again, some of the emigrants complained; they didn't want to give up their wealth. But they had to get over the last mountain, and many of the oxen were too weak to pull the wagons up the steep grade ahead of them. Trading was their only choice.

Perrin approached one Indian girl about his own age who seemed to be in charge of about sixteen horses. He was surprised that she spoke English quite well. "No," the girl was saying firmly to one of the settlers, "one horse for one cow."

The settler swore and slapped his hat against his leg. "That's too much. There are a lot of horses out here in this country. We saw a herd of wild horses just a few days ago. But there are very few cattle. Cows are worth more than horses. I want two horses for one cow."

"Go catch your own horses and break them if you can," said the girl. "But right now, I have horses, and you need them. As for your cows, they might die before I get them home, so I'm taking a risk even accepting them in trade. My price is firm."

"You're just a wisp of a girl, and there's only a few of you blasted Indians. We could take those horses and run you off with nothin'," shouted the settler. A couple other pioneers gathered around and chimed in. "Yeah, we want a better deal," and, "You Indians charged us too much for that flour, too. We could get it for half that price back east. You're trying to cheat us!"

Perrin smelled trouble and ran off to find his uncle. By the time they got back, more pioneers had joined the crowd and were yelling at the girl, but she had not backed down. Finally, Marcus Whitman stepped in. "You have no cause to complain about the price of that flour," he told the settlers. "Flour's cheap back east because it's plentiful. Out here we're talking about the first few fields of grain ever planted in Oregon. These Indians might need it for food this winter. You should be grateful they're willing to sell it to you at all."

"If those heathen wouldn't sell it, we'd just take it," came a voice from the back of the crowd.

"And who'd be the heathen then?" shot back the doctor. "Now you all calm down. I don't mind you bargaining, but there's no need for threats. You either pay for what you want or go without. Don't forget you aren't over these mountains yet. Besides, you're going to want these Indians as your friends, not your enemies."

Most of the settlers nodded in agreement at Whitman's words, but one man piped up: "We're our own friends. We don't need any Indians as friends. And if they make trouble for us, we can defend ourselves."

"You have no idea what you're saying," corrected Marcus Whitman. "There are more Indians in this country than you imagine. You *do* need them as your friends. Now either trade for these horses or clear out."

Several of the settlers drifted away, but a few remained and traded with the girl with no more bullying.

Perrin stuck around watching as the girl pointed out various qualities of the horses she had to trade. Some were exceptionally strong. Some were young. Some were easy to manage. Sometimes she got a cow for a horse. Sometimes it was a couple sheep. Sometimes she got an oxen and a bolt of bright cloth.

The agreement was that the settlers would continue to drive the livestock along with the wagon train herd and deliver them in payment at Waiilatpu.

When the trading was over, Perrin spoke to the girl. "I'm Perrin Whitman," he said admiringly. "What's your name?"

The Indian girl smiled. "Shikam Pitin. It means *Horse Girl* . . . but you can just call me Shikam."

"Where'd you learn to speak English?"

"At the mission schools in Waiilatpu and Lapwai."

"Waiilatpu! Then you must have gone to my Aunt Narcissa's school. Doctor Whitman is my uncle. We've

come all the way from New York."

"And I have come over the mountains to sell my father's horses."

"Looks like you did a good job. Who's your father?"

"He is a chief of both the Nez Perce and the Cayuse, Chief Tuekakas."

"Why didn't he come to sell the horses?"

"Because he knew I could do it . . . and because he had to go to Waiilatpu. There is much trouble there."

Trouble? Perrin remembered his aunt's letter. At Perrin's urging, Shikam told him about the fire and the three-day council and Mr. White's laws. Even when the shout went out to move the wagon train, the two young people rode along together and talked. Perrin kept asking questions about things that had been happening between the whites and Indian tribes.

That night around their campfire, Perrin told his uncle about what he'd heard. "Hmm. If there's that much trouble, I've got to get home right away," said Marcus, frowning. "This slow wagon train will take another week or two, but . . . if I rode on ahead, I could get there in a couple days."

"But who will guide the settlers?" asked Perrin.

Marcus Whitman's forehead furrowed in thought. "Chief Stickus could guide them," he finally said. "He knows the way. The question is whether the settlers will follow him." The doctor stood up. "But Chief Stickus is our answer. I'll go ask him now. The settlers will just have to follow him. There's no other way. I *have* to get back to Waiilatpu."

Chapter 6

Waiilatpu: Place of the Rye Grass

RELUCTANTLY THE WAGON TRAIN LEADERS agreed to let Chief Stickus guide them over the mountains. Perrin and Doctor Whitman left at first light to return to Waiilatpu. With them rode the young Indian girl, Shikam Pitin, who was eager to return to her family. Chief Stickus agreed to deliver the stock she had obtained by trading her father's horses.

The three traveled light and rode hard. Though Perrin had been in the saddle all day, every day, for the last three months, he was not prepared for how grueling such a hard ride could be. Each rider brought an extra horse, and they traded off every couple hours so that

67

the animals with a load could have a rest.

Perrin's second horse was one of the Indian ponies. It was strong and surefooted, but its gait was much rougher than the big bay his uncle had bought for him from the family that stayed behind at Westport. Perrin's legs and back were soon aching, but he pressed on anyway.

"The wagon train won't come this way," said Perrin's uncle. "It's much too steep . . . they'll probably go around the steepest mountains and come up the south fork of the Umatilla River. But it's shorter for us to go right over these ridges."

Whitman led the two young people on faint Indian trails through fragrant pine forests and then out into open alpine meadows with only an occasional gnarled cedar or juniper tree. Unlike fallen trees at lower elevations, which rotted away and soon disappeared into the ground, dead trees on the high mountains lay above ground like the bones of ancient dragons bleached white by the bright sun. Perrin thought it looked eerie—like an ancient burial ground.

The horses continued to scramble up rocky ridges until the trio was riding the very backbone of the Blue Mountain range. Then, just at sunset, as they rode over the five-thousand-foot summit, Perrin sucked in his breath. The majestic view that spread out before him was like nothing he'd ever seen before. From the very edge of the trail the mountain fell off steeply to the great Walla Walla valley below, veiled in the blue-gray mist of evening. Beyond it—

some forty miles away—could be seen an immense dry prairie through which cut the silver ribbon of the Columbia River reflecting the setting sun.

Piercing the horizon some two hundred miles away rose a string of magnificent peaks: Mount Hood . . . Mount Adams . . . Mount Saint Helens . . . Mount Rainier. *It's so rugged, so wild, so free,* Perrin thought. *So this is the far west.*

Before the darkness could rise from the valley to catch them on the treacherous trail, the travelers picked their way down the mountain until they came to some sheltering cedars and camped there by an icy spring bubbling from the rocks. The little party's crackling fire in the crisp night air made their meal of smoked venison and biscuits seem like a feast. It was the first time in months that Perrin had made camp away from the clamoring, dusty wagon train with its thousand emigrants and five thousand horses and cows, oxen and sheep. The peace of the mountains worked a magic in him that left him speechless. And after the hard day's ride, neither his uncle nor the Indian girl had much to say.

They stared into the glowing embers until Shikam and his uncle fell asleep. Perrin stirred the fire one last time and curled up under his blanket.

The next morning was so cold that a tin cup of hot coffee and the small fire they had built to boil it did nothing to drive the stiffness from Perrin's bones.

"Let's get going," said Doctor Whitman. "We can get warm on the trail." But even though riding down the steep mountain path was hard work, Perrin did

not shake the chill until the sun came over the mountains to warm his back.

❖ ❖ ❖ ❖

Waiilatpu was just what its Indian name meant: place of the rye grass. The tough green grass was up to the horses' knees and swayed in the breeze like waves on the sea as the three riders plowed ahead, fording the beautiful Walla Walla River three times as they rode across the valley to the mission site.

But Shikam's mind was not on the familiar village she was approaching. It was still swirling with impressions from her trip over the mountains to meet the wagon train. She had never seen so many white people before. In fact, only when two or three villages gathered to fish for salmon each year had she ever seen that many Indians in one place.

What did the coming of all those white people mean? Where would they settle? What would they do? To Shikam, they were not a good-looking people. Their skin was pale and their faces were thin and worried looking. They never laughed and often seemed angry. Maybe it was just that they were very tired . . . Shikam wasn't sure.

She nudged her horse faster so she could ride beside the white boy. "Why do you come here?" she asked Perrin.

"I've come to help my uncle with the mission."

"But there is no mission anymore."

"What do you mean? Uncle Marcus just said that's the mission over there." Perrin pointed a mile ahead to where the mission buildings could be seen.

To Shikam, the buildings didn't matter; it was

the people who made the mission. "But Mrs. Narcissa is gone, and there is no more school. Everything is broken."

"Then we'll fix it," said the boy with an easy shrug.

"But why do all the other white people come to Waiilatpu? Surely it does not take so many to fix the mission."

"No, no," Perrin laughed. "They're farmers. They'll go down to the Willamette Valley and settle there."

"But Doctor Whitman wants us to make farms here. What if the white people decide to make farms here too?"

"I suppose a few might, but so what? There's plenty of land . . . say, is that where you live?" He pointed to the cluster of Indian tepees not far from the mission buildings.

Shikam searched for her family's tepee but did not see it. "I don't see my lodge. Maybe my family has not come from Lapwai yet." Shikam realized that her father would not be expecting her to arrive this soon. He would be expecting her to come with the wagon train, which could take another week or more to arrive.

She wanted to ride on with the doctor and his nephew to find out how they were going to "fix" the mission, but she was afraid that Doctor Whitman would be angry when he saw all the damage that had been done. "I must go and find my family," she finally said and took off at a gallop toward the Indian village, her extra horse trailing along behind.

"See ya later," called Perrin.

Anxiously scanning the village tepees, Shikam still did not see her family's lodge. Didn't her father say that he had to go to Waiilatpu because of some new "trouble"? Had something happened to him along the way? What if he had fallen from his horse and been hurt? As good as Chief Tuekakas was on horseback, there was always the chance of an accident. It wouldn't take much. Shikam remembered how her cousin had been crossing a creek when his horse threw him. His head hit a stone and he had drowned in nothing more than ankle-deep water.

Shikam slid off her pony and wondered what to do. She thought about praying to God for her family's safety, as Mrs. Whitman had taught her to do in the mission school. But the missionary woman was gone now, and Shikam was not sure whether her God had gone away with her or had remained to care for the Indians who believed. Shikam was worried and confused. Maybe she should appeal to the mountain spirit or the wolf spirit and beg them to not harm her family.

As the Indian girl led her ponies into the village, she saw a small crowd of Cayuse gathered on the far side of the tepees. Curious, Shikam headed in that direction. A group of both men and women were gathered around a stranger—an Indian from another tribe wearing white man's clothes: cloth pants, boots, and a red and black shirt. He had on a brown round-topped hat with a single eagle feather sticking up from it.

"I do not lie!" the stranger was saying angrily as Shikam got close enough to hear. "I, Joe Lewis, have seen with my own eyes what the white man has done all the way from the great salt sea where the sun rises to the plains where the buffalo run. Wherever the white man comes, he kills the Indians and takes their land."

"We have driven them off," spoke up the bad-tempered Chief Tilaukait, who was part of the crowd. "Doctor Whitman left his wife and went to the East. We scared Mrs. Whitman, and she went to Fort Vancouver. They will not come back."

"Don't be so sure," sneered Joe Lewis. "One of these days they will come back, and more will follow them until they overrun the whole land and there is no place to hunt and fish."

"Let them come," scoffed Chief Tilaukait. "We will chase them away."

"What if they bring soldiers? I have heard that this Doctor Whitman went to get soldiers. Then what will you do? My own people, the Iroquois, were once a great nation, but they could not stop the white men when they came in great numbers. If the white man does not kill you with soldiers, he will poison you."

"How do you know they will take our land?" asked a familiar voice. Shikam jerked her head toward the speaker. It was her father! She had not seen Chief Tuekakas standing off to her side. The rush of happiness she felt, knowing that her father had arrived safely, was cut short by Joe Lewis's scornful reply.

"Because all they want is land. They have used

up the land in the East, and soon they will come here wanting your land. I have come to warn you!"

Shikam elbowed her way over to her father's side. But even as she slipped her hand into his, she thought of the huge number of white people who would soon arrive. They weren't soldiers . . . but was it true they had used up the land in the east and that was why they had come west? Perrin, the white boy, had said most of them would go on down to the Willamette Valley. But there were so many! If even a few of them stayed at Waiilatpu, their farms might cover the whole valley. Maybe this Joe Lewis was right. Maybe the white people were to be feared.

"Doctor Whitman has returned," she whispered to her father. He nodded slightly, but his thoughts seemed far away.

Shikam looked up at her father's troubled face. She began to worry about having traded horses to the settlers to help them over the mountains. What would Joe Lewis and Chief Tilaukait do if they knew that a thousand whites were about to arrive at Waiilatpu?

Chapter 7

Showdown with Chief Tilaukait

WITHIN A WEEK, Perrin and his uncle—with the help of Chief Tuekakas, his daughter, and a few other neighborly Indians—had cleaned out the mission house, repaired some of the broken furniture, and put most things back in order. Marcus Whitman sent word to Fort Vancouver, and Narcissa was expected any day.

Doctor Whitman believed the best way to deal with the trouble that had occurred while he was gone was to ignore it—pretend that it hadn't happened. "After all," he said to Perrin while they were repairing the broken windows, "there is no excuse for William Gray poisoning the melons. That would make anyone angry. As for what else happened, a few braves just got out of hand. I don't think most of the Indians are that upset. I'll tell Chief Tilaukait that I expect him to keep his braves in line."

The missionary stopped and wiped his sleeve across his sweaty forehead. "What we need to do is get everyone together to make peace again."

"Why don't we have a big celebration dinner when Aunt Narcissa returns," Perrin suggested. "We can invite people from the village—that would show we want to be friends."

Marcus laughed. "That's a great idea, Perrin. See? You are useful to me already!"

Chief Tuekakas, Chief Tilaukait, and several of other headmen were invited to Narcissa's homecoming. At first Chief Tilaukait refused, but he grudgingly said he would come when Doctor Whitman agreed that he could bring a visitor . . . an Iroquois Indian named Joe Lewis.

Perrin asked if Shikam might come as well.

"I don't know," answered the doctor. "This is like a pow-wow. Usually only headmen take part in such events . . . but if the two of you stay in the background, I guess she can come. But mind my word, I don't want either of you to interfere with anything."

A few days later, everything for the homecoming celebration was ready. A steer had been butchered, and all the other food had been gathered. It would take only a few hours to prepare the feast once the doctor's wife got home.

It was a beautiful day in early October, and a crisp breeze foretold the coming of autumn. In midmorning, a wagon driven by a man from Fort Walla Walla rumbled up the road to the mission station, carrying Narcissa Whitman and four orphans she had been caring for—children of white settlers who had died with no relatives to care for them. The trip up the Columbia River by boat had been difficult because of the strong winds that blew down the gorge, but in spite of the long, tiring trip Narcissa arrived with a big smile for her husband.

Marcus was overjoyed at the reunion. "Start the fires to roast the beef, then run to the village and let everyone know we'll have the feast later this afternoon," the doctor instructed Perrin.

Perrin hesitated. He was being hurried off to run errands before he even got a chance to greet his aunt. He had heard she was an attractive woman, but he hadn't really expected her to be so pretty. Her hair was brushed back into a knot at the back of her head, making her dark eyes stand out, wide and friendly.

Fortunately Narcissa spoke up. "And who might this lad be, Marcus? I hope you haven't brought me another orphan to care for! But this young man looks quite old enough to take care of himself."

Marcus laughed. "That he is, Narcissa. Don't you recognize my brother's oldest boy? This is Perrin Whitman. He was just a little shaver when we came west, but he sure did grow up, didn't he now!"

Narcissa smiled warmly. "Welcome to Oregon, Perrin."

Perrin felt his neck grow hot and knew he was blushing. Why did adults always have to comment on how much he'd grown? It was as though they didn't think growing was normal. Nonetheless, he managed to step forward and politely shake his aunt's hand. "Pleased to be here, ma'am." To his embarrassment, his voice squeaked.

❖ ❖ ❖ ❖

The homecoming feast began in the late afternoon. Marcus Whitman and the wagon driver from Fort Walla Walla sat on the ground in a circle with the Indian headmen, while Narcissa and the children sat nearby at a table that had been brought out from the mission house. Perrin and Shikam sat on the ground away from the circle but close enough to hear much of the conversation.

Doctor Whitman asked if the hunting and fishing was plentiful this year. He commented on the crops that some of the Indians had planted, but said nothing about the trouble that had happened while he was gone. Though he had been with the Cayuse Indians for seven years, he spoke their language only poorly and often used an interpreter, so the conversation moved along slowly.

"I'm pleased that the mission crops are doing fairly well, since there wasn't anyone here to attend to them," Doctor Whitman said.

"What crops?" said Chief Tilaukait in his rough English.

"Why, the corn and wheat and potatoes—the crops that William Gray planted in the spring."

"And where would those crops be?" the chief asked, looking around at some of the other Indians. He had returned to his native language.

"In our fields," said Whitman, pointing over his shoulder with his thumb.

For the first time, the visiting Indian, Joe Lewis, spoke up in English. "Those are Indian fields," he said.

"You are mistaken. Those are mission fields," explained the doctor patiently, putting a large piece of beef into his mouth. He smiled at the newcomer as he chewed. "We've been working those fields for several years now."

"But you never paid for them," challenged Joe Lewis. The translator repeated his words in Cayuse and several Indians grunted in agreement.

Doctor Whitman frowned as if frustrated by a troublesome child. "Of course not. Why should we? We did the plowing and planting and harvesting."

"Because," explained Joe Lewis, folding his arms across his chest and glaring at the missionary, "when the Reverend Samuel Parker came through this country asking if the Cayuse and the Nez Perce wanted missionaries to come here, he promised that you would either rent or buy any land that the mission used."

"I've never heard of such a thing," Whitman protested. "We've always been here at the invitation of these people. My preaching and doctoring is payment enough. Reverend Parker never promised anything more."

"Yes he did!" declared Chief Tilaukait. "I heard him with my own ears."

"I told you!" said Joe Lewis triumphantly, looking around at the other Indians. "The white man comes and makes many promises, but in the end he takes your land. Soon more will come and drive you all away."

Perrin had been listening closely to this debate, but he was distracted by Shikam, standing beside him and tapping him on the shoulder. "Look! Look!" she said urgently, pointing across the valley.

Perrin couldn't see anything.

"Get up. Get up!" she urged.

Perrin stood up and looked over the heads of the seated men. There in the distance a long line of wagons were snaking their way through the tall rye grass. Men on horseback were already breaking away from the front of the column and galloping across the valley toward the mission. They were waving their hats, and even as Perrin watched, he could hear them yelling their greetings.

It didn't take long before the men sitting in the circle on the ground heard the wagon train coming, too. "You see? I am right!" shouted Joe Lewis, leaping to his feet. "They are coming even now to steal your land. You have waited too long to rid yourself of the white devils. Now they will steal everything from you, and then you will die."

Chief Tilaukait and several other Indians took one look and stalked away angrily. The rest of the headmen milled around anxiously, speaking to each other in low tones. In the confusion, the welcome meal for Narcissa Whitman was totally forgotten. As evening descended on the valley and the emigrants began to arrive, Marcus Whitman offered the food intended for a peace celebration with the Indians to the first white arrivals. Then he tried to introduce the wagon train leaders to the gawking Indians, but the Indians backed away and stood silently in a group while wagon after wagon pulled in and made camp.

Soon the entire area around the mission was covered with wagons, campfires, and bawling cattle. White people were everywhere, and the Indians drifted back to their village, many of them convinced that Joe Lewis's predictions had proven true: A few white people had brought more white people, and soon there would be no land for the Indians.

❖ ❖ ❖ ❖

During the next two days, more and more wagons arrived until the entire caravan and its thousands of animals were camped at Waiilatpu. Doctor Whitman tried to encourage the Indians to trade with the emigrants. "Sell your extra corn and grain," he urged them. "Trade horses for cattle. This is your chance;

you can get rich." A few did as the doctor suggested, but most just watched the settlers from a distance.

Doctor Whitman sold so much of the mission's supplies that Narcissa was upset and feared that they wouldn't have enough for winter. "Don't worry," her husband assured her, "we can get more from the Spaldings in Lapwai."

Business was brisk, but some of the settlers balked at the prices Whitman charged. The doctor was selling wheat at a dollar a bushel—twice the price they had paid in the East. "Look," he tried to explain, "it costs more to raise grain out here. Our mill just burned down, and if I need a new harness or a new plow, it has to be shipped all the way across country. And you know how far that is. It's expensive, so I have to charge more."

In the middle of this exchange, an Indian squaw pulled on Doctor Whitman's sleeve. "Please, doctor . . ." she said in Cayuse. "A woman is having a baby. Come quick!"

"A baby?" said Whitman, distracted. "Really, I can't come right now—can't you see I'm busy? I'm sure your midwives will do an excellent job. After all, women have babies every day."

The woman left, and the dickering went on. A few settlers still grumbled that Whitman was unfair, even though the doctor gave away grain and other supplies to families who couldn't afford to pay anything.

❖ ❖ ❖

Three weeks later, most of the emigrants had moved on, but Chief Tilaukait was not reassured. One day Perrin saw him deliberately turn his horses loose into Doctor Whitman's unharvested cornfields. "What are you doing?" Perrin yelled. "The horses will trample and eat the corn. Get them out! Get them out!"

Whether Chief Tilaukait understood all of what Perrin was saying, he couldn't tell, but the chief understood enough to stand by the edge of the field repeating, "My horses. My corn. My horses. My corn."

When Perrin tried to drive the horses out, they only dodged away from him, knocking down more corn. Finally, he gave up and ran to get his uncle.

When Doctor Whitman and Perrin returned, the chief was gone, but the horses were still there. Together the boy and his uncle finally succeeded in driving the horses out of the cornfield and back toward the Indian village. The missionary said, "Come with me, Perrin. We've got to get this settled."

They found Chief Tilaukait sitting in front of his lodge, peacefully smoking a pipe.

As soon as the doctor found someone to translate, he demanded, "Why were you letting your horses trample my corn?"

The chief stared ahead for a long time, and the doctor knew it was best to wait patiently. Finally, the chief said, "The land is ours. Anything growing out of it is ours, so I can feed my horses on it if I want to. If you send any Indians who work for you to drive out the horses, I will whip those Indians. This is our land. What have you ever paid for it?"

The argument continued. The doctor claimed the Indians had said nothing about payment when the mission was first established at Waiilatpu, and the crops belonged to whoever did the work; the chief said that Reverend Parker had made a promise to pay for land the white people used. "All white people lie," charged the chief.

Seeing the debate was not getting anywhere, Whitman turned around and walked away. Perrin followed, looking back nervously. Somehow it seemed rude to just walk away from a chief when he was talking to you. But the man wasn't being reasonable.

"Perrin," the doctor said as they walked back to the mission, "I want you to guard the cornfield every day until we get the corn harvested. It'll be easier to keep those horses out of the field than to chase them out once they get in, but if you have any trouble, come get me immediately."

Trouble came the very next day. Perrin had fallen asleep under a small cottonwood tree on the edge of the field. He had an old single-shot squirrel rifle across his knees, hoping to shoot a rabbit or other small game. About noon, he was awakened by the thunderous noise of horses galloping directly toward him. The boy jumped to his feet and fired the rifle into the air, hoping to turn the animals away. Fortunately, the startled horses wheeled and galloped away, but following them was Chief Tilaukait and three other Indians.

It was obvious that they had intended to drive

the herd right through the corn, and they were very angry that Perrin had gotten in their way. One of the Indians jumped from his horse and ran toward Perrin with his war club raised high in the air.

Perrin turned and ran as fast as he could toward

the mission. He knew he couldn't outrun men on horses, but that never crossed his mind as he crashed through the door, yelling, "Uncle Marcus, come quickly. Help!"

All four Indians were right behind him. Tilaukait and one other carried rifles; the brave who had run after Perrin still had his war club raised in the air, and the fourth Indian carried an ax. Hearing the commotion, Doctor Whitman came into the room.

Chief Tilaukait pointed his rifle right at the doctor's chest and said, "You leave Waiilatpu! Go now!"

Doctor Whitman stood in the middle of the room without moving, and Perrin felt as if time had ground to a halt. Then, calmly, the doctor called to one of the friendly Indians who often worked around the mission. The Indian came into the house, and the doctor asked him to translate. Then Doctor Whitman stared hard at the chief and said, "If you and your people hold a proper council and decide that you want us to leave Waiilatpu, we will go . . . but not because you run in here with a gun pointed at me. Now get out!"

Then, without saying another word, the doctor turned his back on the Indians and walked out of the room.

Perrin stood rooted by the fireplace as the chief and those with him looked at one another. Chief Tilaukait scowled at Perrin and stomped out of the mission house, followed by his companions.

They hadn't been able to break Doctor Whitman's will . . . yet.

Chapter 8

The Fate of Yellow Serpent's Son

ALL THROUGH THAT WINTER and into the next spring there were small incidents that Doctor Whitman and Narcissa believed were the work of Chief Tilaukait or the troublesome Tomahas. Tools were stolen, windows broken, and some animals disappeared. Once someone cut the tendons on the back legs of a mission cow, crippling it so badly that the doctor had to shoot her to put her out of her misery.

And then, for some reason, the trouble seemed to stop. The chief and those who agreed with him still refused to come to the church services that the doctor held, but the tension seemed to relax.

When Perrin asked Shikam what had happened, she said, "Who knows? Maybe it's because Joe Lewis has moved on to another village. Maybe it's because most of the white settlers didn't stay."

A few settlers had stayed in the valley, but they had not set up new farms. Narcissa had adopted five more orphan children from the wagon train, and three families had stayed "temporarily" to help run the mission. The gristmill needed to be repaired, and Doctor Whitman wanted a sawmill built. Also, without the trouble-causing William Gray around, he needed help farming the crops.

Perrin worked hard every day on the chores around the mission and sometimes rode with his uncle as he traveled to distant villages to doctor sick or injured Indians. The missionary welcomed Perrin's company and valued his nephew's quick grasp of the Indian language. With the help of Shikam, Perrin had learned enough of the Chinook jargon—the trade language for all the Indians of the area—to communicate fairly well with both Cayuse and Nez Perce Indians.

But one day as spring was spreading over the valley, Shikam came to Perrin while he was working in the newly rebuilt gristmill. "We are leaving," she said simply.

"Leaving? What do you mean? Why?" asked Perrin. "Doesn't your father like it here?"

"Oh, he likes Waiilatpu. This valley is like our

second home, you know. But he says there's been too much trouble here. The Cayuse are a bad people. He wants to return to the Nez Perce in Lapwai where there is more peace. He became a Christian there and thinks he can learn more about God there."

"But there has been less trouble in the last few weeks. And my Uncle Marcus teaches about God each Sunday in church. Isn't that enough?"

"My father says more wagon trains are coming, and Waiilatpu is right on the way. When the settlers are here, your uncle has no time to teach him or spend time with the Indians. My father will go back to Lapwai and listen to missionary Spalding."

That was unfair, Perrin thought. The Spaldings were 120 miles to the northeast, off the beaten path of the new emigrants and far away from the forts and other settlements. Of course Henry Spalding could spend more time preaching and teaching the Indians, but that didn't make him a better missionary. "If Chief Tuekakas was smart, he would stick close to my uncle," Perrin told Shikam. "He's the leading missionary in the area—better known than Henry Spalding."

"But your uncle is so busy, he can't even doctor the Indians, so how can he take time to teach my father?"

Perrin felt defensive. "What do you mean? He is always doctoring sick Indians. I have gone with him to other villages myself."

"Yes. But last fall when the settlers came through, a Cayuse woman right here in the village died in childbirth. Your uncle couldn't come—he was too busy selling grain."

Perrin was shocked. He had heard that an Indian woman had died, but he didn't know it was because she didn't get medical care. Bewildered, he said, "Well . . . you can't expect him to be everywhere at once."

"No," said Shikam. "He must choose . . . and so must my father."

❖ ❖ ❖ ❖

Several months passed before Perrin saw Shikam again. Then one day she came riding into the valley with three other young Indians and about forty horses. As soon as he could, Perrin wandered over to the Indian village. Would she still remember him? Would she still want to be his friend?

"Perrin," she yelled when she saw him, "we're going to California. Do you want to come with us?"

Perrin felt his spirits lift. Shikam seemed as friendly as before, and her English was even better.

"California? Why would I want to go to California?" he laughed. As far as Perrin was concerned, Oregon was the most beautiful spot on earth.

"To trade and get rich." Then Shikam explained how Yellow Serpent, a Nez Perce chief, had invented a plan to have some of the young Indians drive a herd of horses down to California to trade them for cattle. "They have lots of cattle in California but not enough horses."

"Where'd you hear that?" asked Perrin.

"From some of the fur traders. They go down there because they get more money for their furs, too."

Chief Yellow Serpent had decided to send his son, Elijah Hedding, on the trip. Elijah had spent many years in a Methodist missionary school and could speak very good English. The old chief thought it would be a good way for his son to prove his leadership.

Chief Tuekakas also thought it was a good plan and had agreed to send some of his own horses with Shikam. She had done a good job trading horses the previous fall. A couple other young Nez Perce Indians had brought some of their family's horses, too.

Later that day Perrin told Marcus Whitman about the plan and asked, "Uncle, do you think they'll be able to trade horses for cows in California?"

"Probably so," said the busy doctor as he dipped his pen in the ink bottle. He was writing a letter to Washington about providing more official support for the settlers in Oregon. A few minutes later he laid down his pen and looked directly at Perrin. "However, I've heard the same thing the Indian girl told you about furs going for a higher price in California . . . and that gives me an idea. I have a whole pile of furs I got in trade with some Indians that I haven't had time to take down to Fort Vancouver to sell. If I sent you to California with them, maybe they would fetch a better price."

"Me go to California?" asked Perrin.

"Why not? I know this Elijah Hedding. He's Yellow Serpent's son and a good man . . . only two or three years older than you. It would do you young people good to have something like this to do. I'd just want you back here before harvest and the next wave of settlers."

❖ ❖ ❖ ❖

The next morning, Perrin joined the trading party headed for California, leading two mules piled high with furs. The mules had been left at Waiilatpu the previous fall by settlers who needed fresh stock, but careful nursing over the winter and spring had brought them back to health and strength.

The journey to California was more difficult than he expected. Perrin had no idea they were going so far south, but the Indian youths pushed their horses hard. Two weeks later they arrived at Sutter's Fort in the foothills of the Sierra Nevada range, halfway between Sacramento and Lake Tahoe.

While Shikam and the other Indians were trying to trade their horses, Perrin went looking for someone to buy his furs. An agent in the office of Beemer & Company offered him the same price he could have gotten at Fort Vancouver. "No," said Perrin. "I've got to get more for them than that. I could have gotten that much up north."

"Then you shouldn't have made such a long trip," said the man with a shrug.

Perrin left the office in despair. He had to get a

better price. He tried the store, and then the three saloons, asking everyone he met if they knew of anyone wanting to buy good furs. Discouraged, he finally gave up and had turned back toward Beemer & Company, when a rough-looking man in a tall, battered silk hat caught up with him.

"Hey, kid," said the stranger. "I hear you want to sell some furs." The man had huge black eyebrows and a dark, unshaven face.

"That's right," said Perrin. "I've got two mules loaded with the finest beaver pelts you've ever seen."

"Hmm. Beaver don't bring much anymore," the stranger said, raising first one eyebrow and then the other like they were on a teeter-totter. Perrin had never seen such a facial trick. "The English got tired of their fancy beaver hats . . . but I'll take a look at 'em." But when the man had counted the pelts, he offered Perrin even less than Beemer & Company.

"Look," said Perrin, "you gotta beat Beemer's price, or I'll sell to them. Whad'dya say?"

The man in the battered silk hat rubbed his scratchy chin. "Where ya from, kid?"

"Up north—Oregon Territory."

"You down here by yourself?"

"No. I came with friends."

"You come with those horse-tradin' Indians?"

"That's right. So what?"

"Nothin'. Tell you what I'll do. I'll beat Beemer's price by twenty bucks. How's that?"

"Sold," said Perrin. At last he'd made a good deal.

That night Perrin camped with his Indian companions outside the fort. He went to sleep with a plump little money pouch tucked under his head, confident that his uncle would think him a promising businessman.

The next morning, the trading party got an early start, driving their cattle ahead of them. But they had only gone three or four miles when two riders came charging out of the manzanita brush with their guns pulled and bandanas pulled up over their faces.

"Hold up there!" one yelled.

Perrin and the Indians reined in, letting their cattle drift on up the canyon. "What's the problem?" asked Elijah Hedding, who was the recognized leader of the group.

"This is a holdup!" yelled one of the men. "So hand over your money! You first," he said pointing his six-shooter at Elijah.

Even though the man had a bandana over his face, Perrin immediately recognized the bushy black eyebrows that kept dancing up and down. "He's the fellow I sold my furs to!" shouted Perrin.

"You made your last mistake, boy," the man growled, cocking his pistol and swinging it toward Perrin.

Somehow time seemed to slow down for Perrin. He saw Mr. Dancing Eyebrows pointing his pistol at him and expected it to go off at any moment . . . but out of the corner of his eye, he also saw Elijah reach down and begin to pull his rifle from its scabbard. The rifle was out and starting to come up, when suddenly there was an explosion.

Strangely, Perrin seemed to have time to think: Had Eyebrows fired? Had the slug hit him? Perrin didn't think so because the bandit was still pointing his huge pistol at him, but Perrin automatically looked down at his chest anyway. And then he realized that Elijah Hedding was falling from his saddle. As he fell—seemingly in slow motion—the young Indian held on to his rifle. He landed on his back with a jolt, the rifle fired, and the bullet zinged past the rider with the dancing eyebrows.

Action returned to normal speed, and in a flurry of confusion, the robbers took off at a gallop back up into the red-limbed manzanita brush.

"Great shootin'!" yelled Perrin. "Those guys really hightailed it when you drew a bead on them, Elijah."

But Shikam had jumped from her horse and was at Elijah's side. She was saying something in Nez Perce that Perrin couldn't make out.

"Come on, you two," said Perrin, turning his horse. "We'd better get out of here. No tellin' whether they might come back to finish what they started."

"He's hit," said Shikam in a shaky voice. "Elijah's hurt real bad."

Perrin and the other two Indian boys immediately dropped from their horses and went to their fallen friend. But by the time they got to his side, Elijah's head rolled limply to the side and he breathed his last breath.

Perrin was stunned. How could this have happened! Only seconds ago they were on their way home, feeling cocky and eager to head back to Oregon country. And now . . .

Then Perrin remembered the pistol pointed at his own chest.

"Elijah saved my life," he whispered.

Chapter 9

A Stubborn Uncle

PERRIN, SHIKAM, AND THEIR TWO FRIENDS rode for home as fast as they could push their cattle. But the body of Elijah Hedding, wrapped in a blanket and slung over the back of one of the mules, started to smell before they arrived at Waiilatpu.

"Th-the man was after the m-money I got for the furs," stammered Perrin as he tried to explain the tragedy to his uncle and some of the Indians who gathered to lift the body gently from the mule. "The only reason he gave me a better price was be-

cause he thought he could steal it back up the trail. B-but shooting Elijah was outright murder."

"Now we will see about the white man's law," said Chief Tilaukait angrily.

"What do you mean?" asked Marcus Whitman.

"Mr. White's rules say that whoever takes life shall be hung . . . if a white person kills an Indian, Mr. White is supposed to make justice. But we will see. We will see."

Three days later Elijah White rode in. By then Yellow Serpent, the father of the dead boy, Shikam's father, Chief Tuekakas, and many other important Indians from the area had gathered at Waiilatpu. Even Henry and Eliza Spalding had come down from Lapwai.

Elijah White listened carefully to the story of the robbery and shooting. He asked many questions, some of which made Perrin angry. Mr. White didn't seem to believe that Perrin could be so certain that the robber was the same man who had bought his furs. "I'm sure," protested Perrin. "No one else has eyebrows like him. They're like two big old fuzzy black caterpillars dancing round on his forehead."

"You mean, like Reverend Spalding's eyebrows there?" challenged Elijah White, pointing to the black eyebrows of the visiting missionary.

"No. No," said Perrin. "They looked nothing like Reverend Spalding's eyebrows. They were big . . . big and bushy, and they moved around a lot."

"Well, it's sometimes hard in a moment of crisis to be sure exactly what one has seen," said White.

Then Chief Yellow Serpent stood up, and Perrin sat down. He was seated right beside the trouble-causing Tomahas, and on the other side of Tomahas sat Chief Tilaukait. Perrin did not like sitting anywhere near Tomahas, but when he joined the circle of those meeting with Elijah White, there was no other place.

Yellow Serpent's voice was very quiet, and he talked slowly, stopping frequently while Shikam translated. He told of how strong his son was and how he had gone far away to the Methodist mission school to learn about God. He said he now had no one to follow in his path. Then he reminded everyone that he had been one of the chiefs who agreed to accept Elijah White's ten laws. "And now I look to you," he said pointing right at Elijah White, "to do justice as you promised."

Elijah White knew enough about Indian manners to sit in respectful silence for several moments after Yellow Serpent's speech. But during that time, Perrin overheard Tomahas whisper to Chief Tilaukait, "It is time to kill the whites." Maybe the Indian didn't know Perrin could understand his language so well. Maybe he didn't care. The chief just grunted.

Then Elijah White answered. "I would do justice, Chief, for a terrible thing has befallen your son, and I am very sad. However, it is not that easy. The white people in California are like . . . are like . . ." He searched for his words. "They are like they are from another tribe. I am not a chief among them. I cannot go and demand this man's surrender any more than you could demand that the Spokane turn over one of their people to you."

After Shikam translated, Yellow Serpent said, "You have always told us that your great chief in Washington is over all white men, and that you work for him. Is he not over the whites in California?"

"Well, not really. California is part of Mexico—though I think the United States will get it before long. But for now it's like Canada. I can't just go down there and arrest this man. It's more complicated than that."

Chief Tilaukait snorted. "If a Spokane murdered one of our people, we would demand his surrender. If the Spokane people would not give him over, we would go to war! You are just a lying coward."

A great commotion arose around the circle, with many Indians shouting their agreement. However, Elijah White would not give in. He maintained that there was nothing he could do, even though he was very sorry about the death of Yellow Serpent's son.

"Tonight," muttered Tomahas.

"No, but soon," answered Chief Tilaukait under his breath.

For the first time, Perrin felt real fear. His uncle had dismissed the trouble that had happened when he had traveled back east and picked up Perrin. "I don't think it was that serious," he had said one day when Perrin asked about it. "You've got to understand, I wasn't here, so there was no real authority figure to keep order. Then there was that stupid incident with William Gray poisoning the melons.

No one can blame the Indians for getting angry over that. The gristmill was a big loss, and I'm sorry Narcissa was frightened, but in the end, the Cayuse didn't really hurt anyone. They are basically a peaceful people."

But now Perrin wasn't so sure. Being basically peaceful didn't mean that a people couldn't be pushed too far. And then there were Tomahas and Chief Tilaukait. They obviously hated white people. How far would they go to get rid of them?

❖ ❖ ❖ ❖

The very next day, before Perrin had had a chance to tell his uncle about the threats made by Tomahas and Chief Tilaukait, the first wagons of the fall migration of settlers started to arrive. Within three days, the whole valley around Waiilatpu was covered with dusty, worn-out wagons and tired, sick people.

Most of the children and a few of the adults had measles. They were very miserable, and Doctor Whitman was busy trying to make sure each patient was comfortable and protected against catching pneumonia. Though measles is a highly infectious disease, its only serious danger was if the patient caught pneumonia on top of it. A person could die from pneumonia, so the doctor worked night and day nursing the children, encouraging the settlers, and selling supplies to them.

Again, some were upset with the prices he

charged, but he stuck to his plan. "Next year, after you've cleared and plowed and planted forty acres, bring your harvest on up here and sell it for less," he challenged. "Then you'll know how much it's worth, and if you can undersell me, more power to you."

The wagon train Perrin had come west with had included about a thousand people. The one that began to arrive on October 25, 1844, brought at least fifteen hundred men, women, and children. It was an awesome and frightening sight.

With the arrival of the first wagon, Chief Tuekakas had taken Shikam and the cattle she had traded for in California, and headed back toward Lapwai with Reverend and Mrs. Spalding and some of the other Indians. They did not want to be at Waiilatpu amid all the confusion of the arrival of another wagon train. For this reason, Perrin was surprised two weeks later to see Shikam galloping up to the mission. Her horse was covered with foam and had obviously been ridden at its fastest pace for some time.

"Where's Doctor Whitman?" she panted as soon as her feet hit the ground.

"I don't know," said Perrin. "Probably doctoring some of the settlers. Why?"

"My mother is very sick. She needs him!" The girl was so out of breath that she could barely talk. "My father sent me."

Perrin led her off among the wagons looking for the missionary doctor. When they finally found him, he was not doctoring but finishing a trade of some healthy mules for a weak and weary team belonging to some of the settlers . . . plus a little cash.

But when Shikam told him of her mother's illness, he shook his head sadly and said, "I'm sorry, but there's no way I can make a trip up to Lapwai right now. There are too many sick children here."

"Please, Doctor Whitman," begged Shikam, "it's my mother, Arenoth."

"Like I said . . ." The missionary held his hands up in front of him as though stopped by an invisible wall. ". . . I'm sorry, but I can't come now. How can I make a three-day ride over the mountains to give one woman a dose of medicine when people on my very doorstep are sick?"

"You can't do this!" protested Perrin. "Chief Tuekakas and his family are our friends."

The doctor sighed. "Here, Shikam," he said, pulling a small blue bottle from the bag he carried over his shoulder. "Take this medicine back to your mother and give her one swallow three times a day. It will at least make her feel better."

After Shikam left, Whitman tried to explain more to his distraught nephew. "Perrin, much of the illness the Indians experience comes from diseases they catch from white people, but the Indians don't have any natural resistance to them. The same sickness I can easily cure in whites often kills the Indians. The Indians have observed this again and again."

"Then why isn't it more important to be doctoring the Indians?"

"Because they believe illness is caused by a curse or an evil spirit. The medicine man—and that's what they see me as—is supposed to overcome the evil spirit. If I fail, either I'm too weak to be of any value or they may think that I caused the illness in the first place. Either way, if the patient dies, the relatives have the right to demand the life of the medicine man who failed. This is especially true in the death of important family members of a chief; therefore, I have to be careful."

"But, Uncle, Arenoth is Chief Tuekakas's wife, and he's one of the most faithful Christian Indians. He wouldn't blame you."

"You don't know what he might do at a time of intense grief. It's better this way."

That evening when the doctor finally came home for dinner, Perrin pulled his uncle aside. "Are we in danger of an Indian uprising?"

"No, no. What makes you think that?"

"Well, partly your not wanting to go to Lapwai."

"Look, Perrin. By the time I would have gotten there, the poor woman would probably have begun recovering already on her own. Or . . . or she might have already died. I wouldn't have had much to do with it either way. But in staying here, I can help these children and make sure some of them don't catch pneumonia and die. First things first."

"But, Uncle, you're first of all supposed to be a missionary to the Indians—not to the settlers! The Indians need you. The tension around here is more serious than you realize." Perrin then told his uncle about the threats that he'd overheard at the meeting with Elijah White. "The arrival of more settlers just proves to them that they are in danger of losing their land. The Indians are angry. You can't ignore their needs."

"Only *some* of the Indians are angry, Son . . . just the roguish ones like Chief Tilaukait and Tomahas."

"But they have a lot of followers."

"Maybe a few other troublemakers, but most of the Indians are smart enough to accept the ways of the future. You know, some of them are getting rich by trading with these settlers—at least rich by Indian standards. Don't worry so much, Perrin. Everything will work out. Shikam's mother will probably recover on her own."

But that night as Perrin tossed and turned on his cot, he kept seeing and hearing the determined looks and muttered threats of Chief Tilaukait and Tomahas. He wasn't so sure that the "mission Indians," as the cooperative ones were called, were very committed. He had listened to their talk and how easily they sometimes agreed with Chief Tilaukait's threatening speech.

Deep in his gut, Perrin was afraid things could turn dangerous far more quickly than his stubborn uncle was willing to admit.

Chapter 10

Mad Man and Bad Medicine

JOE LEWIS RETURNED the next day. Perrin saw him just after noon riding slowly through the settlers' camp. A sneer curled his lips as he looked from one side to the other at the wagons with their tired families.

He didn't say a thing, but his defiant look caused first one white person and then the next to stop what they were doing and stare at him as he ambled past.

And then Perrin saw why the people stared. Joe Lewis had painted the left half of his face. It was divided right down the center of his forehead, his nose, his lips, and his chin, and the left half was coal

black with nothing but the white of his left eye standing out. It was truly a scary sight. *This is no good,* thought Perrin.

At the edge of the settlers' camp, the Indian kicked his horse into a full gallop and raced for the Cayuse Indian village. Perrin followed him on foot.

Even before he got to the village, he heard the dogs barking and saw a cloud of dust rising around the tepees. Children and women were screaming and running one way and the other. It was Joe Lewis. He was galloping his horse at full speed in and out between the lodges, around one and then back past another. A couple horses that had been left standing nearby spooked and ran off. Lewis hit a rack with deer meat drying over smoking fires and the rack fell down, dumping the meat into the smoldering coals.

On one turn, his horse caught a tent pole, and the lodge nearly came crashing down. Joe Lewis was screaming and whooping like he was going into battle. Everyone was yelling and milling around in confusion, trying to stop the madman. Finally, one of the braves fired his rifle into the air, and Lewis skidded his horse to a stop.

"What's the matter with you?" Lewis screamed in the Chinook language. "Don't you want your village destroyed? Don't you want your children run over? Don't you like your horses to be run off?"

By that time the entire village had come out of their lodges and had gathered around. Perrin was part of the crowd. Chief Tilaukait stepped forward. "What's the meaning of this?" he demanded.

" 'What's the meaning of this?' 'What's the meaning of this?' your old-woman-of-a-chief asks. You tell me, what is the meaning of *that*?" Joe Lewis screamed and pointed toward the settlers' camp. "You do not seem to care that they are here to destroy your village, run over your children, and run off your horses. Why should you care if I do the same?"

Everyone was silent as Joe Lewis's horse pranced wild-eyed from all the excitement in the middle of the crowd. "They have come to kill you and take your land. You mark my words, you sorry groundhogs. If you sit back and let them come, they will take everything!"

Finally, someone bravely spoke up. "But they came last year and didn't take our land."

"No," yelled Joe Lewis. "They went down to the Willamette Valley and took someone else's land. But when it is gone—maybe this year, maybe next—they will steal your land. But first they will kill you. One way or another, they will kill you!"

Lewis's raving was having its effect on the crowd. The people were getting angrier and angrier. Perrin slipped away before someone noticed that he—a white boy—was in their midst. He ran to find his uncle, but once again, Marcus Whitman dismissed the danger. "Lewis is all talk. He tries to stir up people, but they'll calm down by tomorrow."

Perrin wasn't so sure. That night from his bedroom window he could see a huge bonfire blazing in the middle of the Cayuse village, and all night he could hear drums and chanting.

✧ ✧ ✧ ✧

At the end of the first week in November, the emigrants began to leave. And within a few days, all who were going south to the Willamette Valley had departed. But like the year before, a few families stayed behind, and there was another group of orphans; this time it was the seven Sager children. Their parents had died on the way, and thirteen-year-old John had brought his brothers and sisters on, confident that Narcissa would take them in. She had, of course, but her school was now filled almost completely by white children. Only four Indian children still attended.

Doctor Whitman had new jobs for some of the settlers with special skills like carpentry, and others he allowed to stay because they were too sick to travel or their wagons and money had completely given out.

In all, more than seventy white people now claimed the mission and its surrounding grounds as home. Forty-two of them were children, and eleven of the white people were bedridden—mostly from complications of the measles epidemic.

And then the Indians started getting sick. It began with the four Indian children attending the mission school. They took the measles home with them, and within a week three died. Then the disease spread to their parents and other Indians.

Within another week almost all the Indians were sick, and every day four or five died from complications. In every household, the young and the weak were dying. Chief Tilaukait himself lost two children. There was nothing that Doctor Whitman could do to save them. He, Perrin, Narcissa, and some of the other white people tried to nurse the Indians and bring food to the families where everyone was sick, but many Indians did not want their help. They would not eat any food or take any medicine from the hand of a white person. Perrin found that the most helpful thing he could do was simply keep the fires burning in those lodges where he was admitted.

"It's Joe Lewis again," Narcissa said as the Whitmans sat around their Thanksgiving meal, not feeling very thankful. "He's saying we're poisoning the Indians. He's using what William Gray did when he poisoned the melons to prove that the same thing is happening now, but with far more deadly effect."

"That's foolishness!" said Marcus Whitman. "He knows this is a disease, not poisoning. If he came from back east as he says he did, then he's seen how easily Indians catch white illnesses and how hard it hits them."

"He may know the difference between poison and disease, but he's still making his point . . . and with some truth to it, too," continued Narcissa.

The doctor looked shocked. "What do you mean? How can you say that, Narcissa?"

"I just mean that whether it's poison on a melon or a disease, it still comes from white people. From the Indians' perspective, we're poisoning them, and they are dying as a result."

Perrin spoke up. "I heard Joe Lewis talking about you, too, Uncle, and he brought up that old Indian law about medicine men."

"What law?" asked his uncle.

"You know, the one you told me about the other day—that if a medicine man fails to save people's lives, he might have to . . ." Perrin's voice trailed off.

"Speak up! Speak up, son."

"Well, he said that since so many people are dying, either you are causing it or you are powerless to stop it, and . . . and, in either case, you are such bad medicine that you deserve to die."

"That's crazy. I'm not causing this measles epidemic, and the reason I can't stop it is because the Indians have no immunity to it. That's all. There's nothing I can do."

"But, Uncle, even when you could have helped Chief Tuekakas's wife, you didn't go to her."

"So what? Arenoth recovered, just as I thought. The other day I heard that she was up and around—doing just fine."

Perrin was relieved. Ever since his uncle had refused to go to Lapwai, he had worried about his friend's mother.

"But don't you think we better be careful, Marcus?" urged Narcissa. "Maybe we should go away for a while."

"What for?"

"Listen to Perrin! Joe Lewis is trying to get some of them to kill you, and several may be angry enough to do so. He's saying that you care for the whites and they get well, but you want the Indians to die so the whites can take their land."

Perrin nodded. "I heard him talking just this morning. He says you have magical powers."

"What magical powers?" challenged the doctor.

"He said one day last summer you yelled at a warrior and accused him of taking part in killing a white man down at The Dalles."

"That's right," said Marcus. "He was as guilty as sin, but I couldn't prove it. Besides, that Indian lives over the mountains in another village."

"You mean *lived* not lives!" corrected Perrin. "Joe Lewis says you touched him on the chest, and he died that very night."

"Ridiculous," said the doctor. "That man choked on a piece of dried buffalo meat. Everyone knows that. I had nothing to do with it."

"Marcus," Narcissa said anxiously, "the way he died doesn't matter to the Indians. If Joe Lewis is going around saying you put a curse on him, then as far as they are concerned, your magic powers caused him to choke."

"This is foolishness, superstition! I don't want to hear another word about it!"

But even as the Whitmans argued over their Thanksgiving meal, two hundred Cayuse, nearly half of the Indian village, had already died from the measles.

The next day when Marcus Whitman heard that Chief Tilaukait's third child was sick, he tried to go to him, but the chief cursed the doctor and threatened to kill the doctor. Somehow, the rage in the chief's voice convinced the doctor there *was* danger in the peaceful valley called the place of the rye grass.

That night at the table, he said to Perrin, "I want you to leave Waiilatpu tomorrow. I've heard that the Methodists at The Dalles may be interested in selling their mission. Ride down there and talk with Alanson Hinman and see what you can find out. Don't make any offers, just see if he's interested. Stay for a few days to get a feel of the place."

The Dalles was located along the roughest stretch of rapids on the Columbia River; most canoes and boats had to be portaged around its white water. The area was on the border between territory claimed by several Indian tribes, which made it an ideal trading center and fishing spot. And because of its "neutrality," it had been a relatively safe place to establish a mission. But the Methodists were having problems raising money back east, and were considering closing some of their missions in the Northwest.

"Are you thinking of moving there, Marcus?" Narcissa asked hopefully. "It might be a good idea given all the trouble here."

The doctor turned to his wife. "Let's just say I'm exploring our options. I'll talk to you about it later. For now, I just want Perrin to make this little trip."

Perrin headed his big bay horse toward The Dalles the next morning before the sun came up. A fresh blanket of snow during the night made the landscape look blue in the early light. The clouds were clearing, and the valley sparkled like a wonderland. However, Perrin's joy over the trip chilled when he arrived at Fort Walla Walla. He had no sooner walked through the gates when he saw Chief Yellow Serpent, whose son had been shot on the trip to California. Perrin slid off his horse and walked over to greet the old Indian.

"Hello, Yellow Serpent. I'm glad to see you. Is this a good day for you?"

"It is," he said slowly. "But how is it for you? Is Doctor Whitman dead yet?"

Perrin froze in his steps. "M-my uncle is fine. Why?"

Yellow Serpent looked down, shook his head, and walked away.

Chapter 11

Message of Horror

THE MEANING OF YELLOW SERPENT'S WORDS puzzled Perrin as he traveled down the river to The Dalles. Had Yellow Serpent gone crazy in his old age? Or had he asked that question for a reason? If so, what could that reason be?

Perrin's mind swirled with options: Maybe someone had started a rumor that the doctor was sick. Maybe it was some kind of Indian greeting that Perrin had never heard before. But his mind always came back to the worst option: Yellow Serpent had heard of a plot to kill Doctor Whitman and wanted to know if it had happened yet.

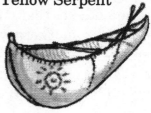

On the first day of December, three days after Perrin arrived at The Dalles mission, a newcomer to the Oregon Territory stopped by, traveling down the river to Fort Vancouver. The man was exhausted from a long trip, but he did not want to spend the night and rest even though Alanson Hinman urged him to do so.

"What's the rush?" asked Perrin as he helped the man load a few fresh supplies into his battered canoe.

"Nothin'. I just gotta get to the fort."

"Why? What's so important that one day more would make any difference?"

"It's none of your business, young man. Just help me push off here," the man said as he climbed into his canoe.

"But, sir . . . you can't take that canoe down those rapids by yourself. The river will swallow you alive. At least let me help you portage it around the roughest water."

"No! No. I want to stick to the river. I don't want any Indians to see me."

"You what?"

"I said, I don't want any Indians to see me making this trip. Now don't ask any more questions."

Perrin shook his head and tried again. "Look. Let me go with you for a ways. I'll take the bow and we can paddle to that outcropping you can see down the river. From there you have only a short portage around the worst of the rapids. The trail goes through some big rocks, so you're not likely to be seen. But it would be crazy to try to run these rapids alone."

Finally the man agreed, and they did as Perrin advised. When they beached the canoe just upstream from the outcropping, the stranger thanked Perrin and admitted that he would have never made it alone; the river was obviously too rough to go any farther. Together they wrestled the craft out of the icy water and dragged it down the snowy path to a place at the river's edge where it was again safe to launch. The water was fast-moving but relatively smooth.

"Thanks," said the stranger.

"Thanks isn't enough," said Perrin as he faced the man, who was only slightly larger than he was. "I want some information from you. What're you up to? Why so secretive? Why don't you want any Indians to see you?"

Reluctantly, the man responded. "Okay. I'll tell you. But I don't want you spreadin' the alarm and creatin' panic."

"Panic about what?"

The man dropped his voice to a whisper. "Well, just two days ago, a chief—I think they said his name was Tilaukait, or something. Anyway, after his third son died—"

"His third son?"

"That's what they said. He and some renegade Cayuse attacked that mission where all those missionaries are—you know, the Whitmans, the ones who help settlers over the mountains. They killed the doctor and his wife and ten other white men."

The man's words hit Perrin like a slap in the face.

Then a numbing horror spread over his whole body. "How . . . do you know this?" he managed to say.

"Heard it at Fort Walla Walla. One of the families escaped and made it there yesterday. But there's not enough men there to defend the fort from a serious attack. Everyone's afraid this will lead to a general uprising among all the Indians in the territory, and the whites have no way to defend themselves. Even you folks down here at The Dalles could be in danger. So we decided to keep the whole thing quiet until we can get enough help to make a stand. They sent me downriver as though nothing had happened—since I was traveling this way anyway. I'm to get word to Fort Vancouver. Maybe they can send back a rescue party."

"Rescue party?" asked Perrin, so dazed and bewildered he hardly knew what was happening.

"Well, there's lots of people still trapped at Waiilatpu . . . mostly women and children, I guess, who were taken captive. There are rumors that even more men—the ones who had been working away from the mission in the sawmill—were also killed."

Perrin stood there in shock. He couldn't say a word.

"I gotta go now," said the stranger. "You keep this quiet, you hear? If those Indians see the whites starting to run around like chickens with their heads cut off, they'll know the word's out, and they might attack so as to get the jump on you before you can get ready or send for help." Then he was off, paddling down the broad, swirling Columbia River.

Perrin's first urge was to ride directly to Waiilatpu. He couldn't believe that such a nightmare had come true! He felt sure his aunt and uncle were still alive. Maybe there had been a little trouble. Maybe someone had even gotten hurt or killed. But a massacre? It couldn't be! He needed to get back and find out for himself.

He ran back up the trail, stumbling over the rocks buried beneath the snow and bouncing off the boulders along the side of the path. When he finally arrived at The Dalles mission house, he was totally winded. He tried to calm himself and catch his breath before he entered.

Maybe the stranger was right about not spreading an alarm. There were only two men at the mission here and only six Hudson's Bay Company men at Fort Walla Walla. So few defenders would make no difference against hundreds of braves if the tribes went on the warpath.

Perrin had to do *something* . . . but first he had to think.

He went deliberately to the barn and started to saddle his horse. He forced his movements to be slow and normal as he filled his canteen and tied his heavy buffalo robe behind the saddle. He would ride out, but he wouldn't panic. He needed a plan.

Slowly it came to him. If the story of the massacre was true, Perrin had to follow the advice of the stranger and not sound a general alarm. There was no way the few whites in the area could defend themselves, and there certainly were not enough of them to launch a rescue of those still trapped at Waiilatpu. Everyone's safety depended upon keeping calm. But there was one possible source of help. The Nez Perce Indians had always been more peaceful and friendly toward the missionaries than the Cayuse. From the very first, the Spaldings had had greater success in converting the Indians of Lapwai to Christianity, and some Nez Perce considered the Cayuse their bad cousins.

Perrin tightened the cinch, swung up into the saddle, and rode out of the barn. He would go to Lapwai, warn the Spaldings, and see if they could appeal to the Nez Perce people to restore peace to the region. Maybe even Shikam's father, old Chief Tuekakas, would help.

It was a dangerous move. If the Nez Perce heard that white soldiers were coming into the area, they might feel threatened. They knew that most soldiers paid little attention to who were the good guys and who were the bad guys when it came to Indians. Many soldiers believed that the only good Indian was a dead Indian. They would shoot first and ask questions later. With that reputation, the Nez Perce might feel that their only safety lay in joining with the Cayuse in a general uprising to wipe out all whites before the soldiers arrived. In fact, Perrin had heard that Joe Lewis had visited several Nez Perce villages trying to stir up followers to run off the whites.

The Cayuse had been shocked at the thousands of whites who had come through their land. What they didn't know was that even more had come by sea and some from California to settle in the rich Willamette Valley. There, they had done exactly what Joe Lewis had predicted: They had driven out the native Americans and taken their land. These whites had come to feel that Oregon belonged to them. Indeed, the issue of "ownership" had been settled between America and Canada, and the Oregonians considered themselves ready to defend the territory from anyone . . . even its native inhabitants, the Indians.

❖ ❖ ❖ ❖

The way over the mountains on back trails in winter was treacherous. The snow had drifted deep, and Perrin was constantly fearful of meeting an Indian war party. The Cayuse certainly would try to rally the other tribes to join a general uprising. If it was true . . . if they'd murdered so many whites . . . their only chance was to defeat them all.

Late in the afternoon, Perrin was working his way down a narrow canyon when he heard a yell behind him. He turned in time to catch a glimpse of three Indians coming down from the rim following his trail. They were too far away to see whether they were Cayuse or not . . . but he wasn't going to wait around and find out.

He spurred his horse on through the deep snow. There was no way he could hide his trail. His only hope was to outrun them. He pushed on. Sometimes his horse broke through the thin ice beneath the snow and dropped into the shallow water of the creek.

When Perrin came out of the canyon into a small valley, he looked back and thought he had outrun his followers. His horse was exhausted, but he pushed him on, dodging between the sagebrush across the windswept land. At the other side of the valley, he rode up the hill a ways and then looked back.

There were three specks following him, maybe five miles back.

When evening came, Perrin's horse was played out. The poor animal was stumbling so badly that Perrin was afraid it would fall and pin him beneath. The boy dropped to the ground. A large moon was coming up. There was light enough to continue, but instead he led his horse into a small grove of cedar trees. He pulled his buffalo robe off the back of the saddle and wrapped it around him as he crawled beneath the thick branches of an old tree. There was no chance for building a fire. It would be a sure giveaway.

In moments Perrin was asleep.

He awoke before dawn from a troubling dream about not being able to get home to his parents in New York, and it took him a few moments before he remembered where he was. He listened quietly to make sure no one was near. Then he slowly rolled out from under the tree, shaking the snow from his robe. Though the sun had not yet come up, the brightness from the snow already hurt his eyes so that he had to squint to see. He looked around for his horse, but it was not there. He whistled, but it did not come. And then he remembered. He had made no effort to tie the animal or hobble it.

He looked for its tracks in the snow and soon saw that they returned to the trail on which they had been traveling. Strangely, the animal had turned and continued on in the direction they had been going. Perrin was surprised that it had not headed back, but maybe it was looking for food or water.

Perrin followed his horse's tracks a few yards and then realized that they had been joined by three other sets of tracks. The Indians who had been following him the day before had passed that way during the night. Possibly there had been enough moonlight for them to see the tracks of his horse but not enough to see that its burden was lighter.

Cautiously, Perrin walked on down the trail, keeping a watch for anything unusual ahead of him. The tracks continued all morning, and then far ahead he saw a dark shape in the snow. He knew he should be more careful, but he was getting so tired and thirsty that he plowed ahead. Once a sense of danger crossed his mind. The area was good for an ambush. There were large bushes and occasional juniper trees, and some unusual mounds of earth.

And then he was at the dark shape. It was his big bay horse. It had fallen dead in the snow, probably from exhaustion.

Perrin stared at it as he slowly moved around to the animal's head. He reached down and felt the body. There was very little warmth left. The horse

had been dead for several hours.

He took his canteen from the saddle and shook it. It was partly frozen. He pulled the cork and sucked water from the slush inside.

The sharpness of the cold liquid revived him, and he looked around more carefully. Tracks showed that the Indians had been there, too. The tracks also showed that they had ridden off to the west; apparently, they had given up following him. They probably figured that he was back along the trail somewhere, as dead as his horse.

That was a good guess. In the middle of this wilderness, in the middle of the winter, there was very little chance anyone could survive on foot. But Perrin was determined to go on. He hiked all the rest of that day and into the night under the bright moon. When he finally fell to the snow in exhaustion, he was too tired to make camp. He slept where he dropped, saved from freezing only by the thick buffalo robe.

When he awoke, there was no feeling in his feet. He tried to stand up, and fell flat on his face. His feet felt totally frozen. Crawling down into a nearby creek bed, Perrin gathered driftwood and brush until he had enough to build a small fire with the flint and steel he always carried. Once the fire was burning, he pulled off his boots. The sight of his feet shocked him. They were stark white except where they had been worn raw. There, the blood and water that had oozed out of the broken blisters had frozen into ice.

Perrin tried not to panic. If he thawed his feet too fast, he might lose them, so he grabbed handfuls of snow and rubbed them on his feet. Again and again he did it until a pinkness began to return. But then came the pain, pain so terrible that tears streamed down his cheeks and he wanted to scream. But they were tears of joy, too. The pain proved that his feet were not dead.

He continued to work on his feet for the next hour until he could hold them near the comforting warmth of the fire without the pain knocking him out. Then he pulled off his shirt and tore it into strips to bind up his feet and protect the raw and bleeding places.

His feet had swollen too much to fit back into his boots until he cut the boots open down the back. He had to tie them on with strips cut from his buffalo robe.

Finally, about noon, he was on his way again, heading northeast toward Lapwai. But by then, walking was terribly painful and exhausting. He could only travel twenty or thirty yards before he had to stop and rest. To help his progress, he cut two walking staffs from a tree. His clothes were torn and frozen in places to his body. The blood from his tortured feet had leaked through to freeze to the inside of his tattered boots.

Night came, and the moon was out when Perrin finally reached Lapwai. His approach brought him first to the Nez Perce village. The mission was beyond. He staggered along a frozen creek bed, intending to sneak around the village. He had no way of knowing whether the Nez Perce were also in revolt or not. But his legs would not go on. He had fallen to the frozen ground so many times that he gave up trying to rise again and crawled to the rim of the creek bed.

There, not twenty yards away, was the lodge of Chief Tuekakas. He was sure he recognized it. Painfully he crawled out of the ditch toward the tepee. If he could just speak to Shikam! She would help him, even if the other Nez Perce had gone to war with the whites.

Closer and closer he crawled. There was smoke rising from the tepee, but the voices coming from within did not sound familiar to Perrin. He did not recognize Shikam's voice or her mother's or little Joseph's voice. He could not hear Chief Tuekakas.

Something was wrong!

He backed away, and with great effort rose halfway to his feet and stumbled toward the creek bed. He fell, rolled over and over, and crawled on his belly until he reached the edge and slid over.

The village dogs heard his commotion and began yapping and howling. They caught his scent and were soon on his trail.

But Perrin could go no farther. He lay still, sobbing quietly in the snow. How long he lay there, he did not know, when suddenly strong hands yanked him to his feet. A knife was at his throat . . . held by a Nez Perce brave.

Chapter 12

The Chief's Protection

Perrin's mind fumbled for an escape. He did not dare ask to be taken to the mission. The Indians might be at war with the whites. Finally, he managed to mumble, "Chief Tuekakas. Take . . . me . . . to Chief . . ."

The Indian grunted and pushed Perrin toward the village, but the boy's legs crumpled under him, and he fell flat on his face into the frozen mud and snow of the creek bank. He tried to rise, but everything went black.

❖ ❖ ❖ ❖

When he came to, he felt a burning sensation on his face. It was dark and something wet seemed to be smothering him. He gasped and tried to sit up. Suddenly, there was light everywhere. He looked around. Several faces were looking at him, and a woman's voice said, "Now there, Perrin. Now you're coming around."

Perrin looked toward the voice and strained to make the face come into focus. . . . It was Eliza Spalding!

She smiled and reached toward his face with a wet cloth. That was what burned so much. His face must be frostbitten.

"Well, son," said the gruff Henry Spalding, "what were you doing wandering out there on a cold night like this . . . and without a horse? And what are you doing up here at Lapwai, anyway? Where's your uncle?"

Perrin realized he was sitting on a wooden floor in a room lit by several candles. Nearby a fire roared in a big stone fireplace. Perrin looked from one person to the other. Kneeling beside him were Henry and Eliza Spalding and Chief Tuekakas. Behind the chief stood a worried Shikam. There were two other Indians whom Perrin recognized as leading Nez Perce Christians: Timothy and Eagle. Finally, Perrin saw the brave who had found him in the snow. The man stood back from the rest with his arms crossed and a deep frown on his face.

"It's . . . the mission," Perrin rasped. His mouth was so dry that it hurt to speak. Mrs. Spalding noticed and fetched him a ladle of water from a bucket on the table.

When he had taken a few welcome swallows, he tried to tell them the story he'd heard of the massacre at Waiilatpu. Eliza Spalding cried out in disbelief and horror; the others received the news with troubled silence.

"I was afraid of this," said Henry Spalding. "There's been trouble brewing here, too. And that renegade Joe Lewis is behind most of it. Perrin, we truly thank you for coming to warn us . . . but now we'd better pack and get out of here."

"No!" said Perrin. "There can't be any panic." He looked around at the group and noticed that the brave who had brought him in from the cold was gone. "I-I think there's only one hope for peace—and that's if the Nez Perce people can be persuaded to stay out of the fight."

"He's right," said Eliza. "And the first thing we must do is tell them what has happened. It is better that they hear it from us along with an appeal for peace. It will show courage and trust."

Reverend Spalding stood up and stroked his bushy black beard. His piercing dark eyes darted from side to side. "You are right. The news will spread fast enough, and if the people hear it from some of the unfriendly Indians, it could be just the thing to inspire further violence."

"I think they may already be hearing it," noted Perrin. "That brave—the one who brought me in— slipped out as soon as I told what happened."

"Chief Tuekakas . . . Timothy . . . Eagle," said Henry Spalding, "would you be willing to help spread the word as fast as possible? Try to get the people to remain calm and not join in with the violence."

The men nodded and left. Shikam managed a smile at Perrin and followed her father out of the room.

❖ ❖ ❖ ❖

The next morning, Perrin was feeling much recovered. Mrs. Spalding's hearty food was improving his spirits as well as his health, but his face had been frostbitten, and his feet were still severely swollen. He was able to hobble around the mission house only with the help of a sturdy walking stick.

Mrs. Spalding insisted that he keep off his feet, so he positioned himself near a window so he could see out. However, what he saw worried him greatly. Indians were positioned around the mission buildings at every hiding place, and they all seemed to have guns.

"Do you think they're getting ready to attack?" he asked Reverend Spalding anxiously.

"I couldn't say," said the missionary. "They're keeping so low that I can't tell who they are, but we better get ready."

The Spaldings barred the door, tipped the table up against one window, and pushed a cabinet against the other. They then piled supplies and beds—anything with weight—against these barricades. "I don't know how much good this will do," said Eliza. "If they want to storm the mission, there's no way we can keep them out for long."

"We must put our trust in God, Eliza," said Henry gently. "He is our one true hope."

About noon there was a knock on the door. "Who is it?" shouted Henry Spalding.

"Chief Tuekakas."

They quickly unbarred the door, and to their relief the chief explained that the gunmen positioned outside were about forty friendly Indians who had volunteered to guard the missionaries. "However, you were right, my friends. There are many Nez Perce who follow Joe Lewis. I have learned that two from this village were at Waiilatpu and may have taken part in the attack."

Eliza and Henry looked at each other.

"But we cannot protect you here," continued the chief. "You will have to leave at dark. We will help you get away."

"But where will we go?" pleaded Eliza Spalding.

The chief shrugged. "You cannot stay here. If you stay, the bad ones will kill you, too. And then the white soldiers will come and destroy our villages and make war on the Nez Perce. I have to think of my people, too."

"How about Bill Craig's?" asked Perrin. Bill Craig was a mountain man who had taken a Nez Perce wife and built a strong log cabin about eight miles from Lapwai. Craig always bragged about how he had built his cabin like a fort. "Ya never can tell . . .

never can tell when you'll need some protection," he
was fond of saying.

"Would you help us get to Craig's?" asked Spalding.

The chief thought for a moment and then nodded. "Be ready at dark."

Eliza Spalding found some old boots of her husband's that would go over Perrin's bandaged feet. The missionaries gathered only a few essential things they could carry. Then they ate a hurried meal and let the fire burn down. They were ready when the knock on the door came.

It was snowing outside, and Perrin realized hopefully it might help cover their tracks. Their departure was none too soon. An angry crowd, with some people carrying torches, could be seen gathering in the Nez Perce village.

But around the fleeing white people darted what looked like dark ghosts in the snowy night. The friendly warriors moved silently from tree to tree as they guarded the missionaries. Perrin managed to trudge steadily in the snow, in spite of his painful feet, but it was nearly midnight when the party arrived at the Craigs' strong log cabin.

The next morning there was still a strong guard of Nez Perce warriors surrounding the cabin even though the chief had left during the night. Slowly, Perrin realized that while they were being protected from renegade Indians, they were also being held captive. Chief Tuekakas was a very smart man. If the white soldiers came, he wanted to have something to bargain for peace with. He could offer to let the white people go if the soldiers would leave. And, since he had not harmed anyone, they probably would agree.

❖ ❖ ❖ ❖

A week later, when Perrin's feet were almost healed, Timothy, Eagle, Chief Tuekakas, and Shikam appeared at the Craigs' cabin. There was more news from Waiilatpu. The count of whites who had been killed was up to seventeen. That included all but two of the men plus Narcissa. The rest of the women and the children were being roughly treated as slaves of the crazed Cayuse.

"We've got to do something!" cried Spalding. "Can't you take your men and ride down there and rescue them?" he asked Chief Tuekakas.

"I have maybe forty braves who would follow, but it would be a death ride, even for the whites at Waiilatpu."

"What do you mean?" asked Eliza Spalding.

"The moment we attacked, they would kill all the whites." Tuekakas stopped and looked very grim. "But that would not be the end. If I went to war, the other Nez Perce would rise up, and much blood would flow between brothers."

Reverend Spalding nodded slowly. "Well, if you can't ride to Waiilatpu, can you at least make sure that the Nez Perce don't join any general uprising?"

"I cannot guarantee anything," said the old chief. "Many of my people have become angry. Much depends on what you do. If you can keep the soldiers from the Willamette Valley from marching against the Nez Perce, maybe I can keep them from going to war."

The missionary scowled. It sounded like a threat. But as he considered what the chief had said, his frown softened. "Yes. I see," he said. "But, like you, I cannot make a promise. There are forty-seven women and children still held hostage. The whites might try anything to rescue them . . . but I will try. However, to have any influence, I must go down to Fort Walla Walla where I can talk to them."

The old chief slowly shook his head. "No. You just write letter."

"But I can't be sure a letter will do it. I can't even be sure they'll believe that the letter comes from me. You've got to let us go!"

Chief Tuekakas frowned and folded his arms. Everyone was quiet as he considered the risk of giving up his "protection." As long as he had the missionaries, he had something to trade for peace if the whites attacked. He looked around the small cabin until his eyes rested on Perrin.

"No," he said in a deep voice. "Instead, I will send Perrin and my Shikam with your letter. He can talk for you. You stay here and pray, missionary . . . pray he talks strong."

Chapter 13

The Road Home

THE SNOW HAD DISAPPEARED from most of the countryside through which Perrin and Shikam had to ride. Perrin was glad for the girl's company and the surefooted Indian ponies. He tried not to think about the terrible journey to Lapwai he'd made on foot two short weeks ago.

They arrived at Fort Walla Walla on the morning of December 19—nineteen days since Perrin had first learned of the massacre— and that very afternoon sixteen Hudson's Bay men beached their boats on the sand by the river and came

ashore. They had set out from Fort Vancouver as soon as they could after receiving the news.

Perrin wanted to immediately deliver Spalding's letter, but was put to work helping the men unload a large supply of goods they hoped to trade for the release of the captives at Waiilatpu. As they were working, a large military man rode up and yelled, "I've been keeping pace with you scalawags as you rowed up the river. Name's Colonel Cornelius Gilliam, commander of the militia of the Republic of Oregon. Who's in charge here?"

One of the Hudson's Bay men stepped forward. "I'm Peter Ogden, Hudson's Bay Company. What's this about a Republic of Oregon?"

The fat man on the horse laughed so that his eyes became little slits. Gilliam had huge jowls that looked even bigger because of the white sideburns growing down his cheeks. His face was red and puffy, almost purple on his cheeks and nose. "Waal," he said, leaning back in his saddle, "since it's been settled that Oregon now belongs to the United States of America, you Hudson's Bay boys are just visitors around these parts. So I don't expect you to know all the ins and outs of what's going on. But us *Americans"*—he stretched the word out like he was trying to rub it in—"set ourselves up a government here in Oregon. We're big on self-rule, you know. Anyhow, we got us a governor and a militia, and I'm the commander of that militia!"

The Hudson's Bay men looked at one another in surprise. It was the first time Perrin had heard that the long-term dispute between England and the United States had been settled, though Marcus Whitman had expected it for some time.

"At your service . . . so to speak," concluded the colonel, laughing again and touching his hat in salute.

"Oh. At yours, too," said Ogden, wryly. "What brings you upriver?"

"Why, to rescue them poor beggars the savages are holding, of course! I come on ahead to reconnoiter. Fifty men'll be along directly—in a day or two. And within two or three weeks I'll have hundreds of mounted volunteers in the field, a real army, I can tell you. . . . Say, could some of you boys come over here and help me get down off this dumb beast? I think she's about ready to collapse."

Two men stepped forward, and with a lot of grunting and groaning, the fat colonel finally succeeded in landing safely on the ground, where he rocked back and forth shaking first one leg and then the other to revive his circulation.

When the supplies had been unloaded, the Hudson's Bay men and the colonel went into the fort and gathered in a room that was hardly large enough to contain everyone. Perrin grabbed Shikam, and they squeezed inside, too.

"Hey. What's this boy doin' in here? And this Injun girl? She could be spyin' on us," barked the colonel as he eased himself down on a keg of nails.

Perrin spoke up for himself. "I'm Perrin Whitman, and this is Shikam Pitin, daughter of Chief Tuekakas of the Nez Perce. She's not here to spy. We have an important message from Reverend and Mrs. Spal—"

"Whitman, huh?" Gilliam interrupted. "You related to the honorable doctor and Narcissa, rest their dear souls?"

Perrin gritted his teeth. "Yes, sir. I'm their nephew."

"Ya know," said the colonel, pointing his finger at the Hudson's Bay men, "every true Oregonian loved them Whitmans for what they did, helping thousands of emigrants to come west." The militiaman continued to dominate the conversation with tales of the great westward migration.

Finally, to Perrin's relief, Peter Ogden turned the conversation to the business of how to save the captives. "We came hoping to do this thing peacefully. Most of the hostages are women and children. I say we try and trade for them. If we attack Waiilatpu with force, I'm just afraid there will be more bloodshed."

"Waal, I ain't afraid of nothin'," boasted the colonel. "With my fifty volunteers, I'll go right in there and clean out that nest of savages in nothin' flat. Just you watch."

"I'm sure you would, Colonel. But in the meantime, what would happen to the hostages?"

"If those savages touch so much as a hair of their heads, I'll burn 'em at their own stake."

Ogden nodded grimly. "I 'spose you'd love trying, Colonel, but seventeen people have already died, and from what I've heard, the whites who remain have already had more than the hair on their head 'touched.' They've been mistreated somethin' awful. We just want to get them out—alive."

"Waal, it galls me to talk of givin' them Injuns anything but a belly full of lead after they killed white people. What you going to trade 'em?" asked the colonel.

"We brought as much as we could load in our boats. I just hope it's enough: blankets, cotton shirts, forty pounds of tobacco, a dozen guns, and six hundred rounds of ammunition."

"Guns and ammunition? Are you crazy?" shouted the colonel. "They'll be shooting it right back at us!"

"Colonel, did you think they had nothing more than bows and arrows? They're already well armed. If we want to free those people, we've got to offer something worthwhile. It's the only way."

Perrin was grateful that the Hudson's Bay men were talking trade—not war. Shikam poked him and he realized it was time to present the letter from Reverend Henry Spalding, requesting that the white soldiers leave the Nez Perce alone, in return for the safe protection of the Spaldings.

"That's bribery!" the colonel protested, but everyone else agreed that the Nez Perce had not been involved. The debate continued to rage for at least an hour.

Finally, Perrin worked up the courage to confront the colonel. "Sir, there are some in the Nez Perce and in all the other tribes in the Northwest who would like to chase all the whites from the territory. If you do not promise to leave the Nez Perce out of this, they will join the Cayuse. If that happens, the Walla Wallas, the Spokane, and the Yakima could join in the fight, as well. There are not enough white people in all of Oregon to resist such a massive uprising."

The colonel looked around. Everyone was nodding in agreement. "Nah . . . there can't be that many Indians around. I don't know whether to trust you Hudson's Bay boys or not. You're obviously on the side of the English and would like to see the United States get the bad end of this stick . . . but I guess your plan does make some sense."

He paused and scratched his sideburns. "All right. If you can get those hostages out by trading, I'll promise to leave the Nez Perce alone . . . unless they put themselves into the fight. But if they start something, then all bets are off."

❖ ❖ ❖ ❖

The peace council with the Cayuse occurred the next day near Fort Walla Walla under a white flag. The colonel couldn't understand why everyone insisted that he stay out of sight. Chief Tilaukait himself attended, even though it was widely reported that he was the leader of the massacre. With him was his son, Edward, who spoke English quite well, and several other leading men.

Peter Ogden was an old hand at negotiating with Indians. He did not rush things. He began by reviewing the honest way the Hudson's Bay Company had dealt with the Indians over the years. Then he reviewed the evil events of the massacre and expressed his shock that the Cayuse would do such a thing. Finally, he offered his ransom for the release of the captives.

The Cayuse were concerned about punishment for the murders they had committed, especially since none of the other tribes had joined them in a general revolt. So Chief Tilaukait presented a counteroffer: "We'll give you the prisoners in exchange for the supplies under one condition: You forget about the killings at Waiilatpu and we will forget about the murder of Elijah Hedding. Then we will all be even and can live in peace."

"I'll pay you what I promised for the hostages," said Ogden. "And I'll do all I can for those who took no part in the killings, but I cannot promise to prevent war. The Hudson's Bay Company is neutral, and the Americans may come and demand punishment for the murders."

Chief Tilaukait frowned. It was not what he wanted to hear since he was deeply involved in the killings, but after all the victory feasts, the tribe's supplies were almost gone. They had no extra food to trade for new blankets or other necessities, and they had shot off much of their ammunition in wild celebrations.

Finally, the chief said, "We do not want war. I will hand the hostages over, but to no one but you."

And so it was agreed.

On December 30, the survivors of Waiilatpu

reached Fort Walla Walla with nothing but the clothes on their backs. The women were worn and beaten, and many of the children—including Narcissa's orphans—were sick. As Perrin and Shikam helped comfort and care for the children, the boy realized it would take years for them to get over the massacre of their parents and the terror of their captivity . . . but at least they were free.

❖ ❖ ❖ ❖

By spring, many things had happened. The Spaldings had been quickly released and had gone down to the Willamette Valley for some rest.

The Cayuse burned the remaining mission buildings at Waiilatpu and then scattered into the hills to hide.

Colonel Gilliam finally commanded a volunteer militia of over five hundred men who chased the Cayuse for a couple months with an occasional skirmish but not much success. One day, however, the loudmouthed colonel pulled a rifle out of a wagon by its barrel. In so doing, the trigger caught on something and he shot himself and died. Many of the other soldiers gave up chasing Indians and returned to their farms for spring planting.

Finally, some regular U.S. Army troops arrived in the territory and continued to chase the Cayuse until the tribe surrendered the five men most responsible for the murders: Chief Tilaukait, Tomahas, and three others. All five were quickly tried and hung. Joe Lewis was never captured, and the Cayuse as a tribe never regrouped but merged into the other tribes in the area.

Perrin Whitman decided to return to his family in Rushville, New York. It was a crisp but sunny day when he rode out, backtracking the Oregon Trail, which was by then deeply rutted from the hundreds of wagons that had come west.

But when he was on the far side of the valley, he decided to take the shortcut over the high mountains, the same trail he had first ridden with Marcus Whitman and Shikam.

Up and up his horse climbed, leaving the valley behind. The grass was turning green on the hillside and leaves were out on the birch. Perrin stopped at the same spring where he and the doctor and his Indian friend had spent their first night. Then he climbed on higher.

At the summit, he turned and looked back. The view was magnificent. Piercing the horizon some two hundred miles away he named off Mount Hood . . . Mount Adams . . . Mount Saint Helens . . . and Mount Rainier. The shimmering ribbon of the Colombia River still cut through the rolling high plain. And below stretched the rippling green sea of Waiilatpu, the place of the rye grass.

Off to one side of the valley, something caught Perrin's attention. It was a rider, someone herding horses. He watched closely. There was something about the way the rider cut from side to side, always keeping the horses together. What amazing skill.

"*Shikam Pitin,*" he whispered, "a real horse girl."
Tears came to his eyes. He believed his uncle had sincerely wanted to bring the Gospel to these Indians, to educate their children, and help them adapt to a changing world. But somehow, Marcus Whitman had gotten distracted by the excitement of westward expansion of white civilization and visions of his own importance. He had indeed become an important actor in the settlement of Oregon by white people . . . but in so doing, the dream of mission work among the Indians had turned into a nightmare.

"But what if," Perrin murmured to himself, "what if someone lived as a friend among the Indians, just to serve them in the name of Jesus . . . putting the Indians first and not trying to make history?"

He watched the rider and horses below for a long time. Then, with a smile on his face, Perrin turned his horse around on the narrow path and started back down the trail to Waiilatpu.

More About
Marcus and Narcissa Whitman

AS MENTIONED IN THE INTRODUCTION to this story, the time was condensed to about a year and a half. The massacre at Waiilatpu did not actually take place until 1847 when Perrin Whitman was about seventeen years old.

Marcus and Narcissa Whitman are not very commendable Christian heroes in the tradition of other Trailblazer characters. They did many things wrongly and may have had wrong motives at times. Their end was tragic, not heroic.

However, their story is an accurate representation of most missionary work among Native Americans . . . that is, until recent times. There may be isolated examples of missionaries who did better in the short run, but tragedy almost always followed.

The main problem was that the American expansion came into direct conflict with Christian mission efforts, and the Indians were caught in between.

Why the Whitmans chose Waiilatpu for their mission location is not fully known. They were warned from the beginning that the Cayuse were not a stable people. But there was tension between the Whitmans and the Spaldings, so maybe it was in a spirit of generosity that Marcus sent the Spaldings north to Lapwai to work with the more responsive and peaceful Nez Perce people. (They, after all, had been the tribe to ask for missionaries.)

Waiilatpu turned out to be right on the Oregon Trail, and the Whitmans quickly got caught up in promoting the settlement of Oregon. To the thousands whom they helped, they *were* heroic pioneers. But not to the Cayuse. However, before we blame the Whitmans too harshly, we should remember that there was no way they could have prevented the westward expansion of America . . . with essentially the same consequences for the Indians.

Not long after the trouble with the Cayuse settled down, Eliza Spalding died, and within a couple years Henry remarried and returned to Lapwai to minister among the Nez Perce Indians. But the troublemaking Joe Lewis had been right all along. When whites came into an area, they sooner or later wanted the Indian land.

In 1855 so many whites were wanting their land that the United States Government called a council with all the Indian tribes in the area to convince them to move onto reservations. The government promised that the reservation land would belong to the Indians for as long as the grass grew. Chief Tuekakas (often called Old Joseph) signed the treaty, but with fear that it would not last.

Indeed it didn't. In 1860 gold was discovered near the North Fork of the Walla Walla River. Within the next three years, many millions of dollars of gold were taken from Indian lands. In 1863 the government decided to reduce the reservation to one tenth of its original size.

Negotiations with the government were difficult, and the Nez Perce asked for Perrin Whitman to be their translator. Old Chief Tuekakas warned his son Joseph that the whites would try to get their land. "This country holds your father's body. Never sell the bones of your father and mother," he said. So the "little brother" of Celia (or "Shikam Pitin," as this story calls her), who was twenty-three years old and a respected chief by this time, refused to be confined to a reservation.

Ultimately, a real war broke out when the government tried to force all the Nez Perce onto the reduced reservation.

Chief Joseph led about half of the Nez Perce people toward safety in Canada. Along the way, they won nineteen battles with the United States Army, but they were ultimately captured just thirty miles from the border. Chief Joseph's leadership was declared brilliant, his military maneuvers some of the most amazing ever performed, but he had never wanted war. All he wanted was to be free to live on the land of his people.

A point of interest: When my (Dave's) Great Aunt Emma Susan Dooley was a girl, she met Celia's brother Joseph. That was after the war, and by then he was known as the famous Chief Joseph of the Nez Perce people. She frequently told of being very impressed by him. She also knew Catherine Sager, one of the orphans cared for by Narcissa Whitman.

For Further Reading

Drury, Clifford Merrill, *Marcus and Narcissa Whitman, and the Opening of Old Oregon* (Glendale, Calif.: A. H. Clark Co., 1973).

Jones, Nard, *The Great Command* (Boston: Little, Brown and Company, 1959).

Lavender, David, *Let Me Be Free, the Nez Perce Tragedy* (New York: HarperCollins, 1992).

Morrow, Honoré, *On to Oregon!* (New York: William Morrow and Company, 1946).

Osinskin, Alice, *The Nez Perce* (Chicago: Children's Press, 1988).

"The Itch to Move West," *National Geographic*, Vol. 170, No. 2, Aug. 1986.

Thomasma, Ken, *Soun Tetoken, Nez Perce Boy* (Jackson, Wyoming: Grandview Publishing Co., 1984).